Don't Take Teddy

by Babbis Friis-Baastad

Translated from the Norwegian
by Lise Sømme McKinnon

AN ARCHWAY PAPERBACK
POCKET BOOKS • NEW YORK

DON'T TAKE TEDDY

Archway Paperback edition published February, 1972

Published by
POCKET BOOKS, a division of Simon & Schuster, Inc.,
630 Fifth Avenue, New York, N.Y.

Archway Paperback editions are distributed in the U.S.
by Simon & Schuster, Inc., 630 Fifth Avenue, New
York, N.Y. 10020, and in Canada by Simon & Schuster
of Canada, Ltd., Richmond Hill, Ontario, Canada.

Contents

Don't Take Teddy

1

The Handball Game

It wasn't Teddy's fault. He couldn't help it. He can't help anything.

We were on fall vacation. Father calls it "spud break" and Mother "tater break," because they both think I should help them in the garden during vacation. They don't understand that things are very different here from where they grew up—Father in the heart of the "spud" country and Mother near the Danish "tater" fields.

At least they'd let me sleep as long as I liked because it was the first day. Now I was sitting alone in the kitchen, eating my breakfast from Father's plate. He'd left early without touching his food, although he'd drunk all his coffee.

Mother and Teddy had eaten. Especially Teddy—crumbs and blobs of jam were splattered among the rose patterns on the oilcloth. A fly was walking about, enjoying itself. Maybe it thought it was in a meadow, sucking honey.

The water pipes hummed and thudded; Mother must be busy in the basement. She probably thought I'd clear off the table, because it was a holiday. Perhaps she hoped I'd wash the dishes too. But I'd promised to dig up the last potatoes, turn over and break up the soil, and burn the rubbish. That was more than enough if I had to look after Teddy at the same time.

I thought I heard someone calling me over the fence. "Mikkel!" What a racket! I pushed open the window and stretched to look over the ivy.

Per and Leif Arne were standing by the gate, and Karsten was behind the gatepost. They began to wave their arms and signal when they saw me. "Over here, Mikkel!"

I shouted at them to come over to me, but they didn't understand, and I couldn't talk very distinctly with a piece of bread in my mouth. So I waved, gulped down the bread with a little milk, and ran outside.

"You'll have to come, Mikkel. The Biters' team is on the field already."

"What?" I wasn't even half awake yet. Why should I go to the field, and what did the Biters' team have to do with it?

"Haven't you heard? We're going to have a re-play. The Biters want revenge. And we can't say No, because it'll look as if we're scared. Hurry up! Bredo has the ball. He's waiting at the crossroads."

"Don't make me deaf." I'd taken in most of it, though, and it was just to gain time that I covered my ears. "You see, it's . . . this vegetable garden. . . ."

"What's that? Veg—don't be crazy."

"I've got to work in the garden today." It wouldn't help to tell the boys about roots and breaking up soil now.

"You *can't*. You *must* come. We don't have reserves. It'll mean we can't play, and the Biters will say we're cowards. You can help in the garden this afternoon."

I told them to stay where they were, and I ran to ask Mother. My friends were lucky; they didn't have to work during their vacation.

Mother was just coming up from the basement. She was climbing backwards up the steep concrete stairs with the clothes basket. Teddy must be holding the other handle—yes, I saw his head. "My, you're a rale smart lad, Teddy." Mother thinks she speaks Norwegian perfectly, but everybody can hear her Danish accent. . . . Oops! Teddy stumbled!

Although Mother tried to hold on and I threw myself at it, the basket tumbled down the steps— with all the clean clothes!

"Ohhh!" Mother folded and slumped over like a punctured tire. She steadied herself against the concrete wall and looked at the sandy clothes. Teddy was kneeling on the stairs, a sweater over his arm.

3

"Ohhh!" came from him, like an echo. Then he crawled up the stairs on all fours. When he reached the top, he cocked his head and glanced mischievously at Mother. He waited, but since she didn't say anything, he smiled broadly. "Teddy c-lever?"

"Hh-yes, indeed." Mother sighed and pulled herself together, as she always does. "You almost made it this time."

I helped her carry the clothes back down into the wash house.

"Will you wait until I've rinsed them again?" she shouted as the water gushed from the tap.

"Y-es, but I was on my way to the field with the other boys."

"What did you say?" Mother looked very pale and tired in the gray basement light. And when I told her about the handball game and the boys who were waiting for me, she turned away and plunked the clothes, piece by piece, into the tub—splash, splash —she didn't seem to mind that she was getting wet.

"I was hoping Teddy could go out in the garden with you today. I have so much to do."

"I know. I promise I'll do the work in the afternoon instead."

Mother didn't answer. Oh, how mean I felt.

"Er—Teddy might come along and watch us, maybe?"

Oh, no, I shouldn't have suggested that! Now I'd fallen in, just like the clothes.

Mother used her sleeve to push away some strands

4

of hair that hung down over her eyes. Was her hair really so gray, or did it only seem gray down here?

"Wouldn't it be too much for you?" She blinked at me sideways, as if she were sizing me up, somehow, while her hands moved a stick around in the tub. "To look after him and play handball at the same time?"

I had to choke down a little voice inside me that wanted to pipe Yes before I squared my shoulders and said, "Oh, no, that's all right. He's been with us before." But we'd only been fooling about then, not playing a real game.

"I don't know. . . ." She turned the stick more and more slowly among the clothes. "The finished aprons have to be delivered to the shop today. And I have several errands to do."

"Then I'll take Teddy with me. Good-bye," I said hurriedly, and scuttled up the stairs; the boys wouldn't wait much longer.

"Please look after him," Mother shouted up to me. *"Look—after—him"* boomed as if she had a megaphone in the basement.

The boys heard her from the road. "Do you have to take Teddy?" Per asked at once.

"Yes, or I can't go."

"Oh!"

"He'll sit still and watch us." I was trying to convince myself and the boys too.

"Sure."

They took it pretty well. It wouldn't have made any difference if I'd told them that Mother was worn out and needed help, or that I'd had a bad conscience since two days before when I'd smacked Teddy. He'd smeared my essay book with his apple core, and I'd had to tear out three pages and rewrite them. I hadn't connected with his ear but with his mouth, for he'd turned as I lifted my hand. Afterwards he'd just looked at me. I couldn't bear to think of those eyes that didn't understand.

But where was Teddy? "I think he went down toward the apple trees," said Karsten. And then I saw him cantering along. He had almost reached the trees. I ran down.

"No, Teddy, stop! No pom-pom now."

"Pom-pom." Teddy laughed and grabbed at a tree trunk, but I managed to pull him away. When the others arrived, I explained how difficult it is to keep Teddy away from apple trees. He thinks it's such fun to shake down the fruit so that it makes a noise like pom-pom on the ground. We sell apples to people in the neighborhood and just keep the ones that are bruised.

"Teddy probably shakes them down so you'll have more bruised ones," Leif Arne said with a grin.

My friends never really understand. But they're kind to him—at any rate, while I'm around.

I asked them to walk on ahead, because Teddy and I always walk slowly. Besides, I was wearing my heavy football boots, although they're practically useless now that the rubber studs are worn flat.

Teddy trotted after me, very pleased. He said, "Play ball" all the time, because that was what I'd

6

told him we were going to do. And everything that begins with "play" sounds like fun to Teddy. He will double up with laughter at the very sound of the word.

I got back from the orchard just in time to give Mother a hand when she came up with the basket the second time. On the whole, I felt like a perfect angel as Teddy and I waved on our way to the road. Mother stood under the clothesline, small and thin like a girl, waving a dish towel. Her hair shone with a reddish color, but it was very faded.

The weather was fine. The newspapers said we hadn't had such an Indian summer for thirty-six years. The temperature usually rose to seventy degrees by the middle of the day.

The children on our road didn't sound as if they were on a "spud break." From behind fences came sounds of laughter and fun, and on the road bikes whizzed past us.

Teddy wanted to stay and "play ball" with Ellen and Bente, who were pushing their doll prams. But they just stuck out their tongues at him and said, "Boo-ee, stupid."

"Can't you see they haven't got a ball? We have to hurry to the field." I fussed and dragged him with me.

We reached the corner next to the large apartment houses and saw some children selling raffle tickets, in aid of "Prevention of Cruelty"—No, I saw they had disagreed over the spelling and written "Save the Children" instead.

When Teddy saw all the delicious things on their table, he pulled me over to it. An old man with a cane had just stopped and greeted one of the boys he knew: "Good morning, good morning."

"Good morning, good morning." Teddy mimicked him in exactly the same voice and quick as a flash reached for a bag of candy. I snatched it from him before he could grab it. The raffle children grinned; they knew about him—most of them.

But the man didn't grin. He waved his cane under Teddy's nose and scolded him. Teddy was naughty and impudent and even wanted to steal from little children.

I tried to say something but was simply pushed away. "Disgraceful." The cane waved up and down again.

Not until the bag of candy had been hidden under the table did Teddy turn his head so that the man could see his face. Then the old man suddenly seemed to be in a hurry. He rummaged through his pockets, found a *krone,* and put it down between a pair of mittens and a clockwork car.

No, he didn't want to wait for his tickets, thank you. He hobbled away as quickly as he could.

We didn't have time for dawdling either, but again we were held up. Some little children were calling Teddy from behind a clump of red currant bushes across the road. "Come here, Teddy, and we'll give you candy. Nice candy, yum, yum."

"No, don't go to them." But I couldn't hold him back. When the children began to suck the candy

8

with loud noises, he tore loose and ran across to
have a look.

A shower of sand, pebbles, and earth fell like hail
over him. The angelic children guffawed and bolted
toward their homes.

Some grit got into Teddy's eyes, so I had to help
him. Anyway, there wasn't any point in running
after the rascals. I couldn't very well beat up such
little children, and I knew from past experience that
it wouldn't do any good to talk to their parents.

We finally reached the field behind the last
block of apartments. The teams were already taking
up their positions. "Left wing, Mikkel," somebody
shouted, pointing at our end of the field. A boy from
the Junior High was going to be the referee.

I made Teddy sit down on a tool box—one that
the builders had left behind, which was filled with
rubbish. "You'll have a good view from here. Now,
don't move."

Teddy smiled and nodded at all the players, as if
he were a specially invited guest of honor. Luckily
nobody teased or bothered him. I'd been a little worried about the Biters, whom we didn't know very
well—they went to a different school—but they were
facing the other way and didn't seem to notice anything.

Actually, Teddy looked almost normal, as he sat
dangling his legs and swaying a little.

Someone called my name again, and I ran to my
position. The referee blew his whistle.

The Biters got the ball first, and did they make it

move! They'd obviously decided to win today. Tufts of grass went flying as they charged.

Bredo managed to snatch the ball. He threw it to Jørgen, who passed it to Leif Arne. From Leif Arne it came to me. But then a dark head got in the way, and we lost it. It would be I who couldn't—

But Leif Arne nipped it back. He threw it backwards over his head toward Bredo. And a Biter caught it! For Bredo had been pushed aside—at least that's what he insisted, and Karsten said so too. The referee, however, hadn't seen a thing and let it pass.

We didn't make a fuss; we only agreed to play even harder. But after that each of us stuck like a piece of adhesive tape to a Biter.

"Get lost," hissed the black-haired boy when we scrambled for the ball. But I hung on, all right.

The Biters had the first shot at our goal, but they got cheated out of it; Per threw himself in the way and saved us.

The ball was tossed back, and the black head bobbed ahead of me again. But the ball just flattened his hair and came straight on. The leather smacked against my fingers.

Don't let go, don't let go! Hooray, I made it!

Karsten? No, he was fenced in by Biters. So I turned and centered to Tor, who was standing almost uncovered.

The ball didn't reach him. Suddenly Blackhair threw himself against me and dug his elbow right into my stomach.

10

I didn't hear the referee blow, because the ground was going up and down in front of me. No, only up . . . then it rose and tipped me over.

"They sure play rough. . . ." "Call that playing? That's fighting."

From what the boys were shouting, I understood that the referee had called a penalty but that the Biters had protested wildly, saying it had only been a collision. Some collision!

Several of us had been kicked too, and now our whole team was pretty angry.

The spot under my belt stopped hurting, and I straightened up and walked back to my position. Blackhair glared at me furiously.

You can bet we blocked each other! Every time one of us got a chance to catch the ball, the other appeared. We were equally good, and that annoyed the Biter more than anything else. He spat and swore, and it was obvious that he would have enjoyed fouling me again.

It wasn't long before the referee blew his whistle. This time the trouble wasn't Blackhair or me but some nonsense in the right-hand corner of the field —where Teddy was sitting.

Was sitting? Had been.

Because now he was leaping around gleefully with the ball in his hands.

How had he—"Wait! That's my brother!"

The blond Biter who was dashing after Teddy turned and stopped, but before I could reach them, someone else slipped ahead of me and took over. Blackhair!

He threw himself on Teddy's back and pulled him down.

Several of the boys on our team shouted at him to let go. "Careful! Stop!" The answer was a scornful laugh that turned into a yell, because now it was *my* turn.

I'd torpedoed him from the side and freed Teddy, but my advantage lasted only a second. Soon we were rolling about on the grass and wrestling in earnest.

I soon realized he was stronger. But I was angrier. He wouldn't manage to pin down my arms—no, he wouldn't!

I tried giving a jerk to get a better hold, but the result was that he succeeded in rolling me over. I can tell you that sharp blades of grass in one's face aren't exactly pleasant.

It didn't make any difference whether I wriggled like a worm in spasms, shook myself, or arched my back—my arms were wrung backwards, more and more. I had to bite the grass to keep from crying out loud. But ask for mercy? Never!

I could hear the referee trying to separate us. "Stop it, boys. Get on your feet so we can continue the game."

Suddenly the ground shook under a heavy fall.

A voice cried out, farther away. At the same moment I realized that my arms and back were free. Then everything was quiet on the field.

I felt numb and didn't turn over immediately.

A drop fell on the clover leaf in front of my nose. The leaf trembled, and turned red. Another drop . . . two . . . three fell, and stuck to my forehead.

I didn't dare look, but I had to.

I saw two wild eyes above a bloody fist.

Something red was oozing out between the fingers, down the Biter's chin and throat.

"Ahhhhhh." He curled up and moaned, rocked from side to side, and cupped both hands over his mouth.

I didn't understand what had happened until the other Biters surrounded Teddy in a threatening ring.

"You threw a stone." "You dirty pig." "You threw that huge stone."

"What? Was it . . . was it Teddy?"

Our team was bunched together, a frightened, silent group.

I managed to join the ring of our furious opponents.

"Stop! Don't hit him. He can't help it—he doesn't know what he's doing. He . . . can't you see? He's ill."

They looked him up and down and snorted. "Ill? Him? Huh!"

True, Teddy didn't look very ill. He stood in the middle of the ring with an amiable smile, as he seemed to listen first to one boy and then to another.

"Teddy's an idiot," someone said behind me. I think it was Karsten.

I've never put it like that, and Mother and Father certainly would never use that word.

The Biters looked at him more closely now. They nodded to each other.

"He must be crazy to carry on and kill people— crazy. Has he run away from his keeper?"

"Yes . . . no, I'm the . . . he's my brother."

The boys nearest Teddy looked as if they hadn't got the message. "Are you nuts? You're not allowed to keep people like that at home. Look what he's done to Stig's mouth. Just look."

I could hardly bear to look at the Biter, who was leaning against the tool box.

He had spat out a tooth; a clot of blood shone on the ground, and there was a white lump in it. His upper lip was split and had begun to swell terribly.

My insides suddenly went so queer, just as if my stomach had dried up all along the edges. And for a moment I couldn't get enough air.

What we'd always dreaded at home, even though we'd never talked about it, had happened at last: Teddy had done something really wrong. He'd harmed someone.

"We've got to get a doctor!" "Call the police!" The Biters shouted to one another, while Leif Arne and Karsten and the rest of our team looked as if they would rather have been somewhere else.

"He should be locked up." "Behind bars." "On a leash." "In a cage . . . in prison!"

I almost wished the Biters would beat me up,

14

because everything they said hurt me much more than if they had hit or kicked me.

Then they gathered around Stig again, and Karsten tugged at my sleeve. "You'd better clear off with Teddy—quickly, before they call the police. He only wanted to help you, of course, but it was too bad he hit Stig so hard."

"Maybe if you run away with him now, they won't say anything," Leif Arne suggested. Some optimist he was.

I dragged Teddy off with me, but they'd obviously say something—no doubt about it.

"Just you wait! We'll have him locked up!" were the Biters' parting words as we reached the road.

2

We Run Away

Teddy trotted willingly by my side, humming one of his "songs" that no one else understands.

"Help me," Karsten had said. Had Teddy really meant to help me when he threw the stone at Stig? If he'd thought it over, picked up a stone, aimed, and hit . . . maybe he *would* get well, then. Only normal people can think out all that.

"Why did you throw the stone, Teddy?" I stopped and stared into his face with its kind blue eyes that both looked and did not look at me and his mouth that smiled, only smiled.

The "song" stuck on one note, "Bom bom bom," with a nod for every "bom," or almost every "bom."

"The stone, Teddy. Like this one." I bent down and picked up a stone from the side of the road. "Why did you throw it? Throw!" With that I threw the stone in a high arc.

16

"B-al-al-all," hooted Teddy with glee, and held out his hands. "Play ball."

Just as I'd thought.

He'd sat watching us throw the ball, and then he'd probably wanted to try it himself. He'd grabbed it when it rolled over to the tool box.

And after they took it away from him, he'd found a stone and played with that. He hadn't aimed at Stig, because if he had he never would have hit him. Nor had he understood what all the fighting was about.

He'd simply thrown the "ball," which just happened to hit Stig's face.

No, Teddy hadn't changed, but now everything else had.

At last all the people who were dying to lock Teddy up had a reason.

They mustn't get Teddy!

Once the police had called on us because some neighbors complained that Teddy had frightened their children.

That's what they said. But it wasn't true! Their children had teased Teddy, tormenting him and prodding him with sticks. He'd tried to run away, but the children had run much faster of course.

They ran in front of him and around him and behind him, making a horrible noise. A couple of grownups came out and asked them if they were afraid of Teddy. Was he frightening them, perhaps?

"Yes," the kids said, pulling faces. "Teddy is so naughty."

17

The parents didn't listen to what I said; they only believed what their little dears told them and called the police immediately.

Father had to promise that Teddy wouldn't go beyond the gate on his own but would always have somebody with him. At that time my parents didn't count me as "somebody," so they probably meant a grownup.

Even now that I'm thirteen, Mother and Father don't like me to have the "responsibility," as they put it. But Mother has nobody else to help her.

"I can manage Teddy perfectly well," I always tell them, and so I've got into the habit of going out with him more and more often.

But this time I hadn't coped with the responsibility at all! I, who had promised Mother to take good care of Teddy, had completely *forgotten* him. Once the game was under way, I'd forgotten that he was even on the field.

So it was all my fault. But the police wouldn't come and take Teddy. At least I'd see to *that*.

On the way home I thought until my head almost burst.

"Flll-ow-her." Teddy stopped and pointed at Iversen's ladder, which was leaning against his wall.

"No, that isn't a flower. Come on." I couldn't stop to play teacher today. It had been the last time we passed Iversen's house that he'd learned to say "flower" instead of "fower."

I'd repeated the word to him at least fifty times while we looked at the sunflowers growing on the wall. There weren't any now, but Teddy must have thought of them. Thought . . .

Wouldn't that make Mother happy! She wouldn't laugh like other people because Teddy called a ladder a flower. She's happy if he seems to remember something. Then she always thinks that he's going to get well.

I decided I'd tell her as soon as we got home—before I said anything about the game.

But even if I could figure out some way of telling her about the disaster, I still dreaded it. I dreaded it so much that I felt empty.

Mother has often said that she couldn't bear it if we had to send Teddy away, and that's how I feel too.

When I was younger, I couldn't understand why Mother and Father were always fussing over Teddy. Why was it so wonderful if he managed to button *one* button in his shirt, when I, who was two years younger, had dressed myself alone for a long time without being praised for it?

Every day things happened that were difficult to understand. I wondered if something was wrong with me. I thought maybe if I tried to be like Teddy they would care more about me.

Then I got slapped and scolded because I'd aped my poor sick brother.

Naturally I got hugged and kissed as well, and deep down I knew they loved me. They just didn't seem to spend as much time loving me, I decided.

I couldn't believe that he'd be ill forever and ever,

19

any more than the Biters had believed me today. But as time passed, I noticed that Teddy remained a child, although he grew physically. Even though I was younger, I was better at everything and had to help him.

Yes, I think from the first time Teddy came to *me* for help, things changed. He became *mine,* somehow. My big little brother.

When I come home from school, he stumbles toward me, laughs, and calls, "Ellik" from a distance. He gives me what he's holding in his hands, pats and prods me. Do any of my friends get that kind of welcome from their sisters or brothers?

The boys feel sorry for me because of Teddy. They don't say so, but I know. But we don't quarrel and fight like other brothers. Teddy's gentle and happy just to be with me. Well, of course, sometimes it doesn't fit in with my plans to take him with me—like today. And he can fuss and hold me up and spoil things until I get irritated—like the day before yesterday. But that's the only time I've ever hit him, honestly! And afterwards I felt so mean, so mean.

Now I felt even worse. I dragged myself up the kitchen stairs and listened for Mother's voice. The clotheslines were full; she'd probably finished in the basement.

I called up the stairs. There was no one there and no one on the ground floor.

She must have left to deliver the aprons. Maybe she was at the shop. I didn't know what to do.

We had to hurry. The Biters had surely phoned by now, and the police would arrive soon. I must take Teddy away. Away from everything.

But where? It was impossible to hide a big fifteen-year-old boy who didn't even understand that he was supposed to hide. Teddy only wanted to eat at the moment.

He was standing in the kitchen, calling, "Ellik," and he had a loaf of bread in one hand. I unlocked the drawer where Mother kept the knives, cut him a thick slice, and buttered it. "There you are."

The school was empty during the vacation, but it was no use going there. Even if a door should happen to be open, the janitor had too good a view from his windows.

"Mick, too," Teddy demanded.

"It's called milk." The words came from my mouth and my hand poured the milk into the plastic mug, but I was really far away.

The factory warehouse up the hill? No, people were still going in and out of it all the time, and I couldn't wait until four o'clock. I mustn't wait at all. Why on earth couldn't I think of a place? Other people had bright ideas when they got into a tight corner—

"Mick?"

"No, milk."

"Mee-elk?"

"Yes, yes, that's right. You are clever." I said the words absentmindedly and hardly noticed that I was

21

speaking to Teddy. But he shook me when he said, "Clever boy, come soon."

What! I dashed to the window, but there was no-body outside. I thought he might have seen Mother, because she usually told him he was "clever" and that she would "come soon" when she had to leave him for a little while.

There aren't many hiding places in a house with only four rooms. We didn't have an attic. The wash house or the store rooms. No, they would search them first.

I heard a car; the tires screeched around the corner. They mustn't come so soon! But luckily the car passed our house.

Teddy sat peacefully at the kitchen table munching at his bread, and I rushed upstairs to my room. We would need money, of course, if we were to go anywhere.

Everything I owned was in a tea box on my writing desk. I'd earned one hundred forty *kroner* from my job in the summer. I was saving the money to buy skis and boots.

For one second—anyway, not much more—I remembered all the hot hours I'd spent carrying boxes and machine parts to the factory, while other boys in my class swam in the sea or went to the country.

Poor Mikkel—I thought of myself as if I were another person. Mikkel sacrificed his sports gear for which he'd slaved and saved just to prevent his

brother from being locked up for life. I almost cried
thinking how noble Mikkel was.

Wham! There was a crack. This time it was *my*
head. I'd collided with the large cottage key that
hung from a row of hooks on the landing. The key
somersaulted down the stairs with heavy chiming
sounds.

I kicked it out of the way. I didn't have time to
hang keys up.

Suddenly it seemed to chime inside my head too.

The cottage. My uncle's cottage!

I certainly knew the way to it. Father and I had
put up a shed for Uncle just after midsummer. We'd
driven down to the village several times for planks.

Teddy and I would have to take the train. . . .
Well, I supposed we'd manage. I had money. Right.
It was just a matter of going. What would we need
to take?

I dived into a cupboard and found Father's rucksack and flashlight. I ran about like a scared rooster
and gathered a couple of sweaters and raincoats.
What else would we need? Toothbrushes. And
Teddy's bear. I couldn't think of anything else—oh,
yes, food!

There were five loaves in the drawer. Mother had
baked them yesterday. I took two—I knew she'd
baked them for Grandma—and some butter.

My scout knife . . . back up to my room . . . and
an extra pair of socks for each of us. And parkas—
we would need them in the hills. Fortunately I

found them on a hook in the hall. We had to get started.

On a sheet of Mother's memo pad I scribbled, *Don't worry. I'm taking Teddy away so the police won't come for him, but I'll look after him better now. Love, Mikkel.*

I put the piece of paper on top of the stove, and then: "Come on, Teddy, we're going for a walk."

At first he resisted.

"Ee-t up your food!" he commanded himself, and bit into the last crust. But he might take half an hour to finish it, so I wrapped the crust in some paper and put it in his pocket. "You can eat it later. Now you've got to be good and come quickly."

He sighed deeply but gave me his hand, and we padded away from our home together.

I led Teddy down the kitchen steps and looked around. Had anything changed outside? No. The sun was shining in my eyes, and it was warmer, but the apples were still hanging on the trees, and the withered grass and rubbish were still waiting for me in the vegetable garden.

Then I must have changed. I felt as if I were in the movies when the picture is changed and you find yourself suddenly in a different scene.

It seemed to me that the little biscuit-colored house called after us and the ivy tried to hold us back with straggly blood-red arms. "Be careful, Mikkel. Don't take Teddy away from his home!"

But if I didn't take him the police would, and that would be much worse.

The house didn't have an answer for that. It just looked at us sadly with its empty glass eye.

Several times along the road I turned around. Other houses are bigger; most of them are more modern. But none, none is as pretty as ours in the fall, for you can hardly see it. From time to time you can see it peeping out behind hedges, trees, and bushes.

Father was the first person to build in the neighborhood, so our garden has had the longest time to grow. Father did most of the work himself, and Mother helped. They moved into the house just before Teddy was born. Neither of us children has ever lived anywhere else.

And now I was running away from home with Teddy! But what else could we do?

It would be safer to take the path through the little rowan wood where there wouldn't be many people. But even the wood, which we know so well, seemed eerie today. The bunches of red berries looked so angry. They hung like danger signals above us. From time to time a cluster would slap my face. "Stop! Go back!"

No, I had to pull myself together and quit feeling I was in a horror movie. Everything was the same.

Teddy had stopped to shake down rowan berries, but they refused to fall, even though he said "Pom-pom" to them.

"Hurry up. We have to catch the bus." But of course it didn't help to talk to him like that. Teddy can't hurry.

If he gets frightened and tries to run, it's like stepping on the gas pedal in a carnival car: the speed doesn't increase more than there is electricity in the motor. And there isn't much electricity in Teddy's motor. He lifts his feet high in the air, but they don't go very far.

At that moment he wasn't even stepping on the gas. He jogged and stood a little, trotted five steps, and stopped again. Each time I had to hold back a twig or branch for him, he stopped and held it too.

"We're going in a car, Teddy. Car! Brrrr." He laughed loudly at my engine noises and tried to imitate them. Some kind of humming noise came out of his mouth, and we droned noisily through the last group of trees.

We had to catch this bus because the next one wouldn't leave for another three quarters of an hour. It would be too late to escape then.

3

Teddy Disappears

When we finally reached the main road, the bus was waiting at the stop, and everyone had boarded it except the conductor. He heaved a baby carriage into the luggage compartment, and then he looked up and down the road to see if any more passengers were coming.

I nodded and waved at him, and once Teddy had caught sight of the bus, had no problem hurrying him along. He more or less dragged me the last few yards.

If only we didn't see anyone we knew. Neighbors might get curious and ask where I was taking Teddy, and later on they might inform the police.

Sure enough! Mrs. Gren from the store for which Mother sews aprons was sitting up front. Fortunately, she was talking to another woman and didn't see me struggling to get Teddy in the back door.

His legs always have trouble with stairs, and the steps were very steep. "Here we go. That's right—fine." The conductor used a hold for people with bad legs, and we were inside.

There was room near the back. I pushed Teddy into a seat, and he pulled himself over to the window. Good, that meant I could hide him a little with my body and the rucksack. Mother, Father, and I always try to hide him when we're among strangers.

But generally Teddy managers to get himself noticed, and now he was already rocking himself on the seat. He rocked and pushed as if he were trying to pick up speed in a swing. At the same time he went on droning as he had in the wood: "Brr-doon-doon . . ." I sank back in relief as the real motor started up and drowned Teddy's voice.

The conductor was a real friend. "One and a half. Right." That was that, and he went on to the next person.

No surprise because a half-fare passenger paid for a great big boy. No glaring as if Teddy were the man in the moon or an orangutan. Not even an understanding smile and a "Say, would you like to play with the ticket?" so that people would turn to look at the sweet child, while I would reach for the ticket, because Teddy can't grasp it. Oh! I knew it all so well.

We drove past my school, and I looked with mixed feelings, as people say, at the low, pale blue building. Not that I usually long for vacation to end, but it was somehow strange to think that the other children would go back to school without me, that I might never return.

In front of the shops further on I saw some familiar faces—Elna from my school and her mother and also Mr. and Mrs. Gundersen. They didn't board the bus, thank goodness, but they were talking eagerly to a group of people. Had they heard what Teddy—

Hey, was that Mother standing in a line in the self-service shop? The yellow sweater certainly looked like hers, and I ducked down just to play safe. But Teddy didn't, of course.

We swung downhill toward the town, and I sat up again to keep an eye on all the cars climbing the hill, but I didn't see a police car.

The bus got more and more crowded, until finally I had to stand up for an old lady, inconvenient as it was.

Teddy held the rucksack on his lap, and that made him so happy that he laughed out loud. He slapped his hands on the canvas and squawked and nudged the lady next to him because he wanted her to join him in the fun. "Tee-hee-hee-hee-ha-ha."

The old woman shook with annoyance, but another, stouter woman who stood in front of me looked even angrier. "There doesn't seem to be any seat for *me*," she informed the conductor. "That big strong boy in the back needs to rest, poor thing."

I shrunk as far as I could into my sweater. Strong indeed! It was better to keep quiet, so that people wouldn't look at us any more than they already were looking.

"Well, it probably isn't easy for him to keep his balance," suggested the conductor. So he *had* noticed.

"You've got something there." The silk coat next to me flapped around my nose. "These spoiled teenagers soon won't be able to stand on their feet."

Thank you very much. Now the whole bus was looking at Teddy. This was what always happened. Even Mrs. Gren, up front, stopped chattering and turned. She twisted and stretched so that she could look over all the heads.

"Oh, it's just the oldest Grabseth boy. He's . . ." She shook her head and made a figure of eight with her hand.

With that, people started to mumble and mutter all over the bus. They turned around, peered over their shoulders, or just glared without pity.

The fat woman looked really offended. "Well, really! Why don't people like that wear a band on their arm or something, so we can see . . ."

She should have worn an arm band herself, that hag.

First she stared at Teddy, then at the woman beside him. "Isn't anyone looking after him?"

"No—I don't know." Oh, yes, she did, she knew, that old woman. The feathers in her hat waved as she stole a glance up at me. She moved to the edge of the seat, so that no one would think she had anything to do with Teddy.

"I'm looking after him," I had to say.

Then they all had something new to glare at. Me.

It's just a matter of bracing yourself, looking at a fixed spot ahead of you, and digging your teeth into your tongue hard. If it lasts a while, you start feeling cold all over and your eyes start watering, and you have to bend down and pretend to search your pockets for the ticket or something.

We go through this all the time, but we never get used to it. We make believe we don't care. We pretend to each other too.

Teddy's the only one who really doesn't care.

He sat smiling and rocking the rucksack, and he had no idea how much I wished I had a blanket to pull over us both.

Some successful escape! Every single passenger on the bus would remember us and be prepared to set the police on our track.

We'd have to hurry when we reached town. If only we could get away from all the people and be left in peace—then we could manage. I'd manage somehow.

I felt as if Father's hand were on my neck. I thought I could hear his voice saying, "Will you really pull this off, Mikkel?" Yes, I must be hearing Father's voice inside me.

Teddy wouldn't leave the bus after we arrived at the railway station. He wanted to go on riding in it.

"Oh, but we're going to ride on the train now. The big train that says tooooooot," I whispered in despair and tugged at a limp arm. We had to get off.

Oddly enough, he gave in. And after I'd struggled with him down the steps—the conductor helped us

31

—Teddy let out a tremendous "toooooot" that made the people in the bus jump in their seats.

"Yes, that's the noise a train makes." The conductor laughed. Well, now the whole gang knew we were going by train, on top of everything else. I was beginning to feel that we might just as well walk into the police station and report ourselves.

I didn't need to turn around as we walked over to the station steps. Everyone's eyes bored into our backs—I could feel them.

Inside the station there were crowds of people lugging heavy suitcases, rucksacks, and bags. I decided it must be easier to lug them than Teddy. I pushed him a little and tugged him a little, but he bumped into everybody and got in people's way, making them angry.

I sat him down on an empty bench next to a wall. I pushed the rucksack onto his lap again and told him to be clever and look after it.

He seemed to understand that. He smiled, grasped it by the frame, and pressed it against himself. He rocked it kindly and carefully, like a mother does her baby.

He's usually quiet when he's supposed to "look after" something for us, so I walked over to the ticket booth alone and got into a line that seemed endless.

I waited, shifting my feet, behind a tough-looking man with a long beard. He was impatient. "This sure takes time. I guess each person must be buying a hundred tickets."

Maybe our train was about to leave. If only I could have shoveled away the whole line and just walked up to the ticket office and asked.

A voice like thunder boomed through the station —the loud-speaker. Police?

"Attention. Your attention, please. Boom boom —train—boingboouirrrllll on track—oooiiiu for departure. Take your seats, please."

Well, at least it wasn't the police. I wondered which train was leaving. It might be ours.

Other people seemed to think so too, for the line got very restless. Heads swung to and fro like tree tops in a breeze; everybody asked everybody else the same question.

Take your seats, indeed! It was all right for him to say so. I didn't have a chance in the world of buying my tickets, collecting Teddy, and making that train.

"Hello—boooiemuuee-ee." Again the thunder. The words were thrown from one wall to another in the large waiting room, and they were all jumbled, so I only caught "Take your seats."

People began to push and shove in the line. I shoved like the men and women behind me but only got squashed and scolded by the tough man with the beard.

Just as I gave up all hope, my turn came. The train was about to leave the station.

"One and a half to Malberg, please. Is that the train leaving now?"

"Uh? Malberg? You want to know when the train

leaves?" The man pulled a ticket out of a machine and stamped it.

"At two fifty-eight. Here you are." He whirled the tickets and my change out to me through a little drawer.

I tossed everything into my wallet and backed away, ready to make a dash for it.

"You've plenty of time, sonny. More than three hours." The man laughed through the hatch.

Ohhh. Two fifty-eight sounded so near, but the big clock on the wall only said a quarter to twelve, and the train wouldn't pull out until two minutes to three. How slow my arithmetic was. I must be nervous or something.

Three hours—more than three hours to kill in this town. The people on the bus would have plenty of time to inform the police about us.

But it was no use staying here. The railway station would be the first place the police would look for us.

There was a train on the nearest track. Suppose we got on it? Anything would be better than sitting here and waiting for the police to find us. I wished we weren't so easy to spot!

I zigzagged in and out among big and small travelers, but halfway to the bench I stopped short. The bench was deserted. Teddy! Easy to spot? No!

The rucksack was lying on the floor, but Teddy was nowhere to be seen. I grabbed the rucksack and shot along to the candy stall, to the magazine booth, to the shoeshine stand, the ice cream and hot dog stands, the flower stand—no!

I dashed out the main entrance, but there was so much traffic that I couldn't see anything. What if he'd walked up to town or . . . what if he'd boarded the train that had just pulled out?

I ran back into the station and found a ticket collector standing near the empty track. "Have you seen a big boy with light brown hair, a blue sweater, and jeans?" I panted and gasped, fighting for air.

"Yes, sure." The man smiled, and I felt suddenly happy. "I guess I've seen at least eight or ten this very morning."

His expression changed when he saw how upset I got. "Nobody's passed this barrier without a ticket, anyway," he called after me.

"Have you seen a boy, a big boy who was sitting on that bench holding this rucksack?" People looked at me and shook their heads or just shook them without bothering to look. They were busy and couldn't care less about a boy who'd been holding a rucksack.

Teddy's gone! My head thudded. Gone!

It was a conjuring trick. Here I'd been wandering around thinking that I had to take Teddy away, and now he was gone. But surely whoever was playing tricks understood I hadn't meant it. Teddy wasn't supposed to be away from *me*.

All of a sudden I realized that he might have been captured! The police might have found him while I was waiting in line. They wouldn't know I was with him, and he couldn't talk. Oh, that would be terrible.

I stared until my eyes stung, went out the main entrance once more to look. Back to the bench . . . a couple of lovebirds were sitting on it. No use asking them!

It wouldn't help to ask the old man in the corner, either. He was sleeping with his chin on his chest.

"Bill! Over here!" A hunter clumped through the waiting room, sporting a gun and feathered hat. He was walking so quickly that his rucksack rattled. He called his dog, a setter which was sniffing around the telephone booth.

"So here's where you are. I've searched all over for you. Did you realize I was going to put you in a crate?" The man picked up the leash that trailed behind the runaway dog. The setter resisted with all four legs and had to be hauled by his master across the hall to the baggage office.

Some people were lucky and found what they were looking for.

I could see a pair of legs in the telephone booth but no head.

But—the awkward position of the feet and the shoes . . .

One, two, three jumps over to the booth, tug open the door—there! Squeezed against the wall with his back to the door and windows was Teddy.

"Teddy! What are you doing here?"

Although I shook him, it was a long time before he turned his head. His face was a pale gray color, and he looked down. At my feet? At something behind them? Oh oh, I should have known.

"Were you afraid of the dog?" No answer, but I neither expected nor needed one. At home everyone knows how scared Teddy is of dogs.

The large setter had probably gone over to the bench and sniffed at him. For some strange reason dogs get suspicious when they see Teddy—they growl and bristle all over.

Teddy, poor thing, had probably moved to the end of the bench, stood up, and run, stiffly and clumsily as always, and the dog no doubt had followed him.

Someone must have left the telephone booth just as he reached it, because otherwise he never would have known how to get inside.

Fortunately, there had been a door between himself and the dog, a door that glided to by itself, or he might have run out on the tracks or into the traffic.

I shuddered and tried to pry his hands loose from the telephone wire, which he was clutching.

"Let go, Teddy, the dog has gone. Look! Nothing dangerous." But he had gone rigid, as he often does when he's afraid. He was stiff as a post all over, and it took me a long time and plenty of "not dangerous" and patting and stroking before I soothed him.

When his fingers finally dropped the wire and he loosened up, he had to get out in a hurry. "Po-po," he said, but I knew we'd never make it across the waiting room to the men's room, so he had to do it in the corner behind the telephone booth.

Please don't let anyone see the long stream running across the concrete floor! It probably didn't matter much. With all the rubbish that was thrown on the floor, they obviously had to wash it frequently.

There are different ways of being afraid. The panic I'd felt while Teddy was lost was nothing like the old slow terror that now returned.

All the people around us might be enemies—even the ticket collector at the barrier. He waved at us. "So you finally found your pal!"

I didn't want him to remember us! I'd been nuts to wander around asking everybody I saw. I gave him a brief nod, even though he looked friendly.

We had to get out of the station—and quickly!

4

Three Long Hours

It was Teddy who decided how we were going to spend the three hours after we'd safely left the station.

I was on the lookout for anything suspicious, and I forgot about him for a minute. In that minute Teddy caught sight of a streetcar.

He pulled his hand out of mine, and who do you think trotted straight into the traffic before I could grab him? You're right—Teddy.

Cars screeched to a halt and hooted, a lady screamed. It was a real gas.

I thought we might as well cross the street, seeing that the traffic had already stopped for us. But after running the gauntlet, I agreed with Teddy that a streetcar was a good idea.

It left as soon as we boarded it. "Baa baa!" it

sang to all the new witnesses who knew where we'd
been and what we'd done.

Relieved at finding myself in another, safer world,
I took out my wallet and waited my turn. This
would be the third time within an hour that I'd
bought tickets. Some record.

Teddy refused to wait but padded along with two
girls and dumped himself on the seat just inside the
door.

The conductress—I guess that's the right word for
a woman—followed him and looked as if she
wanted to say something. Over here! I held up my
hand and rattled the coins, and then she gave in.

While she sold a season ticket to a man in front
of me, Teddy slid sideways down the seat, farther
and farther. Stop, I thought; but oh, no! He went
right on and pushed himself against an elegant
woman with a bouquet in her arms.

"Look out," she seemed to snap as she dug her
elbow into his side and pressed herself into the
corner.

Teddy didn't notice her expression, of course. He
rubbed his back against the slippery seat and chattered a little to himself as he stared straight ahead.

The two young ladies—no, big girls—who'd
boarded the streetcar just before him, sat opposite,
eating plums out of a yellow paper bag. They
nudged each other and giggled.

Girls like that really get me down.

These girls were about my age, maybe fourteen.
And between the mouthfuls of plum that disap-

peared down their lipstick-smeared hatches, I could see them gabbling full steam ahead about Teddy.

I'd bought the tickets, but it was tempting to stay in the back and pretend I'd nothing to do with Teddy. Very tempting. I knew exactly what would happen if I went in and sat down beside him. And Teddy wouldn't mind if they laughed at him. So they might as well laugh.

No, I wouldn't let them.

Nobody was going to laugh at my brother. And I wouldn't let him sit there alone.

The girls screwed their heads around and immediately began to size me up as I walked into the car.

Sure, sure. I *know* I'm no tough guy. I'm small and thin. My nose is pointed and my hair is light red, just as Mother's once was. But there's no law against looking like a fox, is there?

The two plum girls weren't all that beautiful, either. They'd better not open their traps about me.

Teddy's handsome. He has good, kind eyes, not like those two cold pairs of black-rimmed eyes under haystacks across from me. It gave me a pain just to look at them. They were almost as big and round as the plums the girls were stuffing into their mouths.

They glared at me, and I could feel myself starting to blush.

It didn't help to stare at the advertisement that dangled overhead. My eyes still got sort of moist. The girls probably thought I was about to burst into tears.

Of course I could look back at all the shop windows we passed. But suddenly I saw a whole row of windows with nothing but women's underwear in them. I turned even redder and looked down at my feet.

My football boots were black—black and grayish-white and rather worn. Especially the toes. The rubber was curling on them. The laces had once been red. . . . Horrible girls, please glare at something else!

"Not dang'rus, not dang'rus." Teddy was singing and waking everyone up. He sat on his hands, rocking with delight. Maybe he hadn't realized until now that the terrifying dog wasn't sniffing at his pant legs.

But his song nearly made the girls collapse. They dropped the plums on the floor, bubbled and coughed with laughter, peeped at us and at each other, and started all over again.

"He's nuts, all right." She didn't exactly say it in a whisper. "Listen to him singing, 'Not dang'rus, not dang'rus.' " They roared with laughter.

"Whad'ya think he'll do if we offer him a plum? Sit on it?" Explosion.

They stared at us, purple—yes, the color of plums —in the face, hoping for more fun, while they ate and ate out of the yellow paper bag.

It's easy to get angry with people like that— really angry. But I just felt sick and ashamed.

The funny thing was that nobody else on the streetcar seemed to mind about the girls. They all had their eyes on Teddy.

Maybe other people think it doesn't matter if they laugh at sick boys. They probably thumb their noses at men who've lost a leg or an arm or at men who're blind.

Is it any worse to have something wrong with your head? Should I feel ashamed of Teddy? Sometimes I've had the feeling that Mother and Father are. But that's nonsense—they love Teddy. I couldn't make myself believe that I should feel ashamed.

Instead I kept up a sort of silent conversation with the two giggly girls. You and people like you are the ones who're nuts. You've got the machinery to think, but you can't be bothered to use it. Teddy's head is useless for thinking. One, or perhaps more, of the machine parts is missing. Then you can hardly expect the body, which is run by the machine, to work properly.

The awful thing was that I didn't know if my ideas were right. Nobody had ever told me what was really wrong with Teddy. But it didn't make any difference to the plum girls whether my explanations were correct—after all, they didn't know I was lecturing them.

The last plum stone hit the floor, and the girls stood up. They let out an extra giggle right in our faces and wriggled forward to the exit.

When the streetcar had shaken them off and gone rattling on, I shrunk into myself.

It had been cowardly of me, feeble, not to have said a single word. Even though you won't get a medal for it, it's much braver to speak your mind in front of people like that than to jump into the water and save someone who's about to drown.

I probably wasn't big enough to do that, either, I who—

We passed a church that seemed familiar, and then we passed a big park. We were heading directly for the Biters' hill. Only another three or four stops and we'd find ourselves at home!

I dragged Teddy out of his seat quickly, and we tumbled out of the streetcar as soon as it stopped.

It served me right for not bothering to read the sign on the streetcar before we boarded it at the railway station. We might have drifted smack up to the Biters, straight into the hornets' nest!

The nest was probably buzzing and humming at this very moment. Everybody would be talking about the dreadful thing that had happened earlier in the day and the big boy who should have been locked up a long time ago.

"But you're not behind bars and you're not going to be," I said to Teddy as we scrunched across the gravel path in the park.

"Wass-sh handy," he answered, and steered himself toward the fountain.

There was only one person in sight—a mother who was knitting next to a baby carriage.

Then we might as well stay in the park for a while. It was probably safer than anywhere else. But I still scowled suspiciously at everyone who came through the opening in the rose hedge, whether they walked, ran, or strolled. There just might be a familiar face lurking under that blue hat or polka dot scarf.

I didn't bother about the children who darted over the paths, playing tag; they were so small. The older children were in school—the fall vacation starts later in town.

I envied those kids at their desks who had nothing to be afraid of. That's what I actually thought. Pretty unusual for me!

My watch! It must have stopped. No, it was still ticking, but, oh, how slowly. I wore Father's old watch, which he'd given me. Maybe it needed to be fixed. "Run, run," I muttered to the second hand and tried to make out how many times it would have to circle before reaching two fifty-eight.

Teddy was splashing with a stick in the pond, getting himself wet. But he was singing and enjoying himself, and the sun was almost as warm as in summer, so I let him.

I lay down on the grass and squinted up at the trees. In some places the leaves were yellowish and red. Other leaves didn't seem to understand that it was autumn. They must be too green. I laughed at my joke.

Blue sky, yellow leaves. Sky . . . leaves. Leaves, leaves, sky.

I climbed out of myself, up through the leaves and branches, straight into the blue. I dived into the sky, away from all the trouble down on the ground, just flew, flew.

45

"We soar . . ." Leif Arne has the record, but I couldn't remember the words, I just lay there, whistling the tune.

Nowadays it's possible to climb into the blue. Peer Gynt should have known that. We'd read about him at school, and our teacher told us that Peer Gynt used to lie just as I was doing, and daydream. But they hadn't invented rockets, satellites, and space suits in his day. Just imagine how much more fun he could have daydreaming now!

The sun appeared between two branches, and the light became so strong that I had to shut my eyes. First my right cheek felt hot and the left one cold. Then my nose got warm too, and finally my whole face. If the sun's rays hit the next branch, my right side would get cold.

A lot of strange things were whizzing around in my head, but I knew perfectly well that I'd started the whizzing myself, so as not to worry about other things—like how Teddy and I would manage.

That thought was sneaking about underneath the others, though, burning and aching like a bad tooth.

I jumped up immediately when I heard a woman's voice saying, "Well, gracious me. That's terrible! Did it happen today?"

Two housewives, I guess, with shopping bags. They passed me.

I stood up and followed them to see if they were talking about Teddy.

"Yes, they announced it on the one o'clock news," the other woman said.

Had it been announced on the radio? Then we didn't stand a chance.

I tiptoed after them, like a professional shadow. I didn't find out what the women were wailing about until we'd reached the far end of the park. The price of bread. It had gone up again.

Well, at least they made me realize I was hungry.

And so was Teddy! He wasn't splashing with the stick any more. He sat on the concrete edge of the pond, munching a piece of bread. In front of him stood a child, yelling. Two slightly bigger girls were waving their arms and scolding him.

I never should have left him alone, but the park had seemed so peaceful a moment ago.

I sprinted over and tried to explain why "that big boy took the food from Hege, when she'd just put it down near the pond." And why "he doesn't talk, he's eaten it all up, he's naughty—look!"

Teddy had bent forward to pat the child who was crying, but Hege got frightened, toppled over, and yelled even louder with surprise at finding herself on her bottom.

The two "nannies" didn't believe me when I said the boy was good. But they cheered up after I gave them fifty *øre* to buy buns for Hege.

They pulled the child to her feet, took her by the hands, and wriggled off.

The "we'll buy two ice creams and let Hege have a lick" probably wasn't meant for my ears.

I took Teddy over to a green bench that was hidden by bushes.

I opened up the rucksack and took out the food. Oh, if Mother had known we were going away, she would have packed us something really good to eat.

She'd be very worried when she discovered that Teddy and I'd gone, even though I'd told her not to worry in the message I left. Father too, in the evening—if he wasn't told before or didn't come home earlier.

I would write them that we were safe just as soon as I could. After a couple of days the police might get tired of searching for us.

Hi, there was Teddy ambling over to the pond to "wash hands" again. He must have enjoyed splashing.

"Wash-sh first," he protested as I tried to drag him back.

That's right. We'd been brought up to wash our hands before eating. So we both dippped our fingers into the water and rubbed them a little. "Fine. Now we can eat."

I led him back to the bench. I thought he was very clever to remember. Little things like that make Mother so happy.

The loaves smelled like home. Last night, when Mother baked them, I'd stood next to her, sniffing in anticipation.

The slices looked a bit peculiar, because my scout knife wasn't very sharp.

But the taste! Mother's fresh bread with butter on it—I wouldn't exchange it for ice cream or cake.

I saw someone behind the fountain. Through the spray it looked like—looked like—it was!

A policeman in uniform. He must be on our track.

"Sit still, Teddy." I tossed the rucksack behind the bench, rose, and put my hands in my pockets. I decided to stroll away, just as if I were going for an afternoon walk.

"Stroll" sounds so easy. Sort of amble along. But I felt like an old stiff board. Well, then, march. Put one leg in front of the other, one, two, hup. Don't turn around, don't look.

If only Teddy would go on munching and not say something strange or wave at the policeman as he passed.

Had he noticed Teddy and me sitting together? The police had probably been told to look for a big boy who was being taken care of by a small one.

I seemed to hear the voices of all the people who'd noticed us today: "Yes, the two of them were on the bus going to town." "Got off at the station." "Rode on the streetcar to the hill. That is, they didn't go up to the top." "No, they suddenly got off when the streetcar stopped near the park. . . ."

I imagined someone drawing a circle around the park on a map and giving orders to police car number such and such, and rattle, rattle, they would come with handcuffs.

I'd walked to the end of the path. I couldn't stand glaring at the blasted rosehips much longer. I kicked a stone, turned a little . . . and looked back.

49

The policeman was standing near the pond, and he'd removed his stiff hat. He held his hand under the fountain, rubbed his forehead with it, shook the water off his fingers, and found a handkerchief. He dried his hands and face with it, and peered at Teddy.

And Teddy just sat and stared at me. Typical! Why can't you look at something else, Teddy? He'll see me if you don't.

But the policeman put on his hat, brushed some drops off his sleeve, and trudged toward the exit near the kiosk.

Teddy called, "Ellik!" but the policeman didn't turn around. So he wasn't looking for us!

I could feel my knees shaking as I walked over to Teddy. And Teddy also seemed restless. He fussed and wanted to leave.

It was twenty after two. The time had passed quickly, after all. We had to return to town at once.

The streetcar we caught was rather crowded, so I stood out on the platform and tried to make Teddy clutch the pole in the middle. Every time the streetcar went around a curve, however, he lost his balance and almost fell, and the people next to him had to steady him.

Not all of them were friendly or helpful. I could hear grumbling. I was so afraid of meeting anybody I knew that I hardly dared look up.

But I did see a little. That man with the light coat, for instance, who was just folding up his paper—wasn't he staring at us over his glasses?

And the lady in the gray suit with the basket on her lap—she might be Stig's mother or his aunt.

I nearly had a fit when a big man pulled himself onto the platform and roared over my head: "Well, so here you are!"

But he'd simply caught sight of a friend, one whom he'd tried to phone all day, he said.

Teddy nodded and laughed while the two guys joked and slapped each other. I just managed to hook Teddy's arm before he tried to slap the shoulder of the woman next to him.

She was nice. When she saw a couple of empty seats, she said, "You two go inside and sit down. I'm getting off soon."

I clutched Teddy and pushed him, but we nearly keeled over several times. My arms felt cramped after holding up his heavy body as we went around the curves. I was sweating too, and it was good to sit down and rest.

We had no more scares on the way to town.

Teddy sat quietly. He only let his lower lip hang a little and aired his tongue from time to time.

But it didn't matter because there wasn't a single girl in the whole streetcar!

I half expected to see a reception committee on the steps of the station, consisting of Mother, Stig's parents, police, doctors, and I don't know who else.

But I didn't see anything out of the ordinary.

"Come on, Teddy, we're here," I said, relieved; but Teddy wouldn't budge. He was tired of moving, and the streetcar was comfortable.

I struggled to get him off. The conductor poked his head in and asked, "Well, are you getting off or aren't you?"

A couple of grownups wanted to help me, but Teddy slumped down in the seat, and it was impossible to move him.

"Shall we carry him out between us?" The conductor looked helpless.

I was about to give in and say Yes, because the streetcar was about to leave, when I saw a hot dog stand near the steps!

"Hot dogs, Teddy. Come, and I'll buy you a hot dog."

Yes, it helped to tempt him with his favorite food. Now he did what he was told. He stood up and followed me, crowing like a streetcar bell: "Hotdo, hotdo, hotdo."

Then he thought of something and stopped in front of a man who was sitting near the door. He raised his forefinger and said, "No, ho-ot-do-o." He nodded with every syllable, the way I do when I try to teach him.

The man and the other people on the streetcar laughed. At first. But then someone suddenly said, "Poor soul."

With that they all pulled long faces.

When the streetcar left, I felt as if a funeral procession were staring at us.

They needn't look so sad, I thought.

At home we can always tell if people are laughing *at* Teddy or if they're just laughing because they think Teddy's cute. We often laugh at him ourselves. But this shocks our visitors, and then Mother and Father look serious too.

This time Teddy didn't get a chance to wriggle away from me and run into the traffic. I held his hand tightly and forced myself to watch nothing but the cars and streetcars streaming by us.

Teddy would have his hot dog—two if he wanted them—even if the whole world was out looking for us.

"Two plain hot dogs and one with the works," I said, and stuck up my nose. Nobody was going to suspect that I'd anything to fear.

The woman in the big white apron certainly didn't suspect us: "Uh? One with the works?"

So I had to explain. "One hot dog with mustard and ketchup and onions. And two hot dogs plain, please."

Teddy spills his food if it's runny.

I didn't actually want the hot dog. After all, we'd just finished eating. But I forced it down the hatch, as we wouldn't get any dinner.

Teddy was in seventh heaven, and he smacked and licked his lips as we trotted again into the dear old waiting room.

The station clock, like my watch, said eighteen minutes to three. That meant it was time to board the train. It was a good thing we already had the tickets.

But where had I put them? They weren't in my wallet or my pockets!

I began to feel panicky. Had I really lost those expensive tickets?

I turned the rucksack upside down. No tickets in the side pockets. The back pockets—no tickets.

"Did you take the tickets, Teddy?" He agreed to let me search through all his pockets too, but all I found was a bread crust from our kitchen at home.

So I'd have to buy two more tickets. What a mess! We didn't have a lot of money anyway, and this would mean forty *kroner* down the drain. More than forty *kroner!*

The line looked just as long as it had the first time, and I'd have to take Teddy with me. I couldn't leave him alone.

Then the loud-speaker thundered over our heads, and this time I didn't have to wonder which train was being announced. I *knew* it was ours.

What could I do? We'd never make it.

5

Mrs. Breden Understands

My fingers trembled as I opened my wallet to get more money.

And there were the tickets inside a folded bank note!

What a crazy idiot I was! Teddy seemed to think so too. He was grumbling about being dragged all over the place. He just couldn't understand why we were in such a hurry.

He was still hard at work chewing his hot dog; eating takes all his energy.

I had to be mean and snatch the hot dog from him. I danced ahead and waved it as they do in cartoons, and he followed me, trying to grab it.

People laughed and pointed at us. I couldn't blame them, but I didn't think it was funny.

I suppose it wasn't surprising that the ticket collector recognized us at the barrier—just bad luck. Everything was going wrong.

"Have a good journey." He smiled. Perhaps he noticed that Malberg was stamped on the tickets.

"Go jump in the lake," I mumbled at the kind man. He probably heard me.

I was sorry I'd said it a moment later. I'd never seen such high steps! Teddy couldn't lift his feet high enough to board the train, so we could have used the help of a big strong man.

"Up. Up!" After several attempts I managed to heave him up onto the first step. But that was as high as he'd go. He got down on his stomach and kicked, trying to crawl.

Two suitcases with a man and woman between them came toward us. The couple looked a little surprised to see Teddy's legs thrashing, and chose another door.

When they'd put all their luggage on the train, the man came over to give me a hand. He gripped Teddy under his arms, and together we pulled him into the corridor.

"Did you hurt yourself?" asked the woman, peering at us from the opening between cars. Teddy stood up, and she uttered a little "Oh!" and backed into her luggage.

"Thank you very much for helping me, sir," I said with a bow.

"Don't mention it, don't mention it." The man nodded and backed away too, but he nearly stumbled over the connecting plates as the train gave a jerk.

I could hear doors being shut, and I ran to shut our door. Then the train rolled past heads and waving hands, past a pile of crates, pillars, new stalls, a fence . . . and out of the station.

If only I could find an empty compartment so we could sit in peace.

But there were people in all of them, and the people didn't look as if they wanted visitors. I kept away from compartments with children and teenagers in them and took Teddy into one where there were only three grown-ups.

A bald man and his rather fat wife sat in the seats next to the window. Or was she his mother? No, surely she was his wife.

Their daughter was quite a "dish," as Leif Arne would put it. She sat on the middle seat reading a magazine and didn't seem to notice that anyone had entered.

I put the rucksack up on the baggage rack, and Teddy sat down in a corner by the door, beside the "dish." I dumped myself into the seat opposite him. Oh, what lovely soft seats!

At last I could relax. We were finally leaving the town and everyone we knew. And no one had tried to prevent us! It was too good to be true.

My legs suddenly felt limp. My arms too. They jerked as if a cogwheel were loosening them, notch by notch. My whole body tugged, pulled, and I couldn't make it stop. Every time I started to jerk, I coughed and moved in the seat, hoping no one would notice.

I felt dead and dull inside. I wanted to lie down and close my eyes.

Teddy, however, was in no mood to relax.

He sat fingering the strange door that slid back and forth. He pushed it away, laughed, gave it another push.

Bang! It slammed into the wall on my side. "That's that," I thought, but the lock was obviously broken. The door slid back again, and Teddy waited for it with outstretched arms.

He met it like an old friend, talked to it, and patted the shiny handle. Tchong! It rattled over to my wall again.

The woman next to the window turned—the one who was the man's wife, or mother. "Speak to them, Thorvald. Tell them not to be so noisy."

Her voice and face were thin and sharp, unlike the rest of her.

"Surely you're not going to complain about a door. Train doors are like that," the man barked crossly.

While I peeped at them, Teddy slammed the door as hard as he could.

"No, Teddy. Please don't, Teddy." I held the door, and he shoved and pushed it to make it rattle and bang.

"Oh, Teddy, Teddy," he said and laughed. It was almost like hearing Father's voice when he's fed up but still can't help laughing at what Teddy's done.

But the woman didn't laugh. "You can't let them carry on like that." She didn't talk to us; she was taking it out on her husband.

He hid behind a newspaper and mumbled that boys will be boys.

I looked for something that Teddy could do, something that wouldn't be noisy. Would he like the ashtray on the wall, perhaps? There was one hanging beside him.

"Look at this." I raised the lid. Fortunately, the ashtray was empty.

He forgot about the door and started playing with the lid. He let it fall a couple of times, but he didn't like the noise.

No, thanks. Back to the door and more banging before I could do a thing.

The girl who was reading the magazine slapped it down on the seat and groaned: "Ooohhh, honestly!" And the sour woman attacked her husband again.

"You can't help hearing him, Thorvald. You've got to speak to him. He's got to learn to behave on a train."

"Excuse me, but . . . he doesn't understand." I thought that would be enough, but it wasn't enough for the old hag.

"Well, if you won't do anything, Thorvald, *I* will get the conductor. He can't be far off; he just collected our tickets."

She was about to stand up when her husband bent over and grasped her by the arm. "Keep quiet. Can't

you see he's not normal?" The shiny bald spot
nodded in Teddy's direction.

Both the woman and the girl looked closely at
Teddy. He hammered and pushed to make the door
move, but I was holding his wrist.

After sitting quietly for a few minutes, the sour
woman whispered to the girl, "You shouldn't sit next
to him. You never know what people like him will
do. Come and sit next to me."

She tugged at the girl, who evidently wasn't her
daughter, to make her edge away from Teddy.

The girl shook herself and said, "Honestly" and
"Really" but the woman wouldn't give up.

"He's kind. He's never done a thing . . ." dangerous or bad, I would have gone on, but I swallowed
my words. They weren't true any more.

The woman wasn't listening to me, anyway. She
turned to her husband. "I think you ought to tell the
conductor. Tell him to come and straighten things
out. I don't see why decent people should be disturbed."

But Thorvald slapped the little table between
them, making the newspapers dance. "You should
mind your own business. You're always sticking
your nose in other people's affairs."

Suddenly I couldn't stand them another minute. I
was sick of the quarreling, sick of the people. I
needed air.

I pulled the door open and pushed Teddy into
the corridor.

We stood near a window and looked at the

houses, trees, and bushes whizzing past us. Brown leaves whirled on the tracks and fluttered over the pale, close-cropped fields.

It was good to cool my forehead on the glass pane. I'd have liked to stay there for the rest of the journey, but I couldn't because of Teddy. He was already walking toward a compartment from which music blared.

"Teddy Bear," he called delightedly. To him, all songs are "Teddy Bear," because that's the song we always sing to him at home.

The music came from a compartment two doors away. The door was open, and two girls and three boys, who were about eighteen or twenty, sat inside.

They were having fun, bawling the refrain and swaying to the beat. It made me seasick just to look at them. They obviously found pouring the contents of a bottle into a paper cup difficult, because they spilled a lot on the floor.

A boy lifted his cup to Teddy, who'd poked his head inside, even though I was tugging at his sleeve.

"Hey, pal! Cheers!"

"Come on, Teddy." He didn't listen to my whispers, but only to the music. He swayed to the beat like the others, holding the doorpost tightly as he sang, and laughed at the grinning faces in the compartment.

"Easy, Jensen. If you drink any more, you'll get as high as he is," someone shouted. Laughter.

A yell of delight from Teddy. I couldn't tear him loose.

"How about giving this genius a drink? Maybe he'll go as crazy as Jensen," suggested one of the girls.

"Yesss. Agreed." Applause and enthusiasm.

Luckily Teddy didn't take the cup that was offered to him, as the record ended and the music stopped. I'm sure he wanted to wait for more "Teddy Bear," but when I got really cross, he followed me to the end of the corridor.

The toilet was free, and it was peaceful inside. We drank some water and washed ourselves, but there wasn't enough space for Teddy. His head hit the shelf for the water jug, and at the same time he lost his balance. Oops! His elbow nearly went through the window.

Somebody was rattling the door handle, so we returned to the corridor.

We couldn't walk into the next car. Teddy didn't dare cross the loose connecting plates, which moved separately, and it was a good thing he didn't; they made me think of a roller coaster.

So we stood for a while in the corridor, but we had to flatten ourselves against the wall about once a minute for people who were traveling from one car to the next or going to the toilet.

A man, who'd been smoking in front of a half-open window, walked away, and I quickly took his place.

Teddy gasped at first, but he liked feeling the wind in his hair. I didn't put my head out, but the wind still blew my hair all over the place.

The countryside looked like a picture postcard in full color. We passed a deep blue lake—ultramarine, I decided, remembering my paint box. But I didn't know the right names for all the marvelous autumn colors I saw.

Hey! We were chugging straight into a rock!

We caught a whiff of train smoke and soot and blasts of warm air as the train thundered into the tunnel.

It wasn't long before they switched on the lights in the car, but it was long enough to worry Teddy. "Ell-ik," he squeaked in a loud wail.

I didn't find him immediately, because he'd moved off in the dark.

There. No, I was fumbling at the sleeve of a man.

The train swung out of the tunnel, and I caught sight of him again, but before I could reach him, Teddy fell against a compartment door and hit the floor with a heavy thud.

A woman opened the door at once and bent over him to see how he was.

Teddy was lying still, his eyes open. He really must have given himself a wallop, although he rarely cries when he hurts himself.

A man from the next compartment stepped over Teddy's legs. The conductor walked through the car to announce that there would be a short wait at the next station. Both men asked if we needed help.

"We'll take him into our compartment," the woman said. "There are only three of us in there." Two children jumped down and looked as if they wanted to help, but the men lifted Teddy onto the seat. He filled the whole seat.

"Thank you, we'll be able to manage now," the woman said, nodding. The conductor said we should call him if we had any problems, and the two men left.

I thought the woman was doing quite a lot of managing, but she seemed nice and friendly. Younger than Mother, with light brown hair and eyes that were just right—soft and gentle, the same blue-gray as her sweater and slacks.

"Your brother?" She rolled up a jacket and put it under Teddy's head. I answered before I'd time to think whether it was wise to tell her. But since everybody in the train plus the conductor was probably onto us, it wouldn't matter if she knew that Teddy and I were brothers.

The children stood quietly, looking at Teddy, but their mother lifted the little boy onto the seat next to the window and put a toy on the table.

His sister, who'd lost some teeth and whose hair was braided, was asked to look for the box of cookies in her bag. She found it, and the woman offered me one. "Maybe your brother would like a cookie."

I handed one to Teddy, but he wouldn't look at it.

"Winnipooh," he said.

"What does that mean?" the woman wanted to know.

"He wants his bear, Winnie-the-Pooh. Perhaps I'd better get our rucksack."

64

"Yes, why don't you? I think this is the best place for you."

If only I'd been clever enough to come here in the first place! I recalled passing up the compartment because of the children. But grownups were worse. At least, that couple who'd argued had been.

They were unpacking their food when I went back. I guess they had called a truce. The woman with, not a magazine but a book this time, glanced at me for a split second.

The man was the only person who said anything after I'd pulled the rucksack down from the rack and bowed good-bye.

The conductor was lecturing the teenagers in their "discotheque." He took their bottle away—served them right, too.

It was good to get back to the woman and her children again.

A bit embarrassing, though, to drag the teddy bear out of the rucksack and put it in Teddy's arms. The little boy asked me eagerly if he could borrow the toy.

"No, Peik," said his mother. "The big boy's hurt himself, and he needs his teddy bear to go to sleep." And anyway Peik was going to drink juice from a lovely plastic bottle.

Teddy sighed contentedly and hugged "Winni-pooh" and a little later he closed his eyes and opened his mouth wide.

"Are you traveling alone with your brother?"

"Um."

"Isn't that hard on you?"

"Well—sometimes."

She seemed somehow to know all the answers before I gave them. She'd understood what was wrong with Teddy, I realized, even before he'd been carried into the compartment. And she didn't seem surprised. She made everything seem so normal.

It was so easy to talk to her that I let slip our destination, although I shouldn't have told her.

"Malberg. That's the station before ours," she said. "Then we'll keep each other company all the way. My name is Mrs. Breden."

I did remember not to tell her our surname.

She smiled when I told her our Christian names.

"Teddy and Mikkel sound like something out of a book."

"Nooo, not really. But Teddy's never been able to pronounce his real name, Bjarne, and Mother and Father thought he looked just like a little teddy bear."

"He does," agreed Mrs. Breden. "The name suits him. And you look rather like a fox. Are you foxy?" She looked mischievous now.

What did she mean? Did she suspect that I was running away with Teddy?

"I have the feeling you're a bit sly." She laughed. Then she *knew!*

"Oh, no, don't look so terrified, Mikkel! I didn't mean it like that. Hadn't you better collect the rest of your luggage so you'll have it all in one place?"

"No. We only have this rucksack."

"Oh?" She was waiting for some sort of explanation, but it didn't come. "One rucksack isn't very much."

"I guess not." I felt myself blush. She was embarrassing me like the plum girls on the streetcar, only she was worse—I didn't want to lie to someone who was so nice and kind.

Mrs. Breden didn't ask any more questions. She poured some juice for her children and told them they ought to take a nap like Teddy. "Because we have a long way to go on the train and afterwards we'll have a long drive to the boarding house."

The train had been standing still for a couple of minutes, and now it started to move again, rather unevenly at first, but soon the wheels were grinding out their endless song.

Peik chattered and muttered to himself. The seat rocked up and down when he jumped. But I suddenly fell asleep.

The next time I opened my eyes, I found myself looking down at the bare-rubbed head of the once furry teddy bear. It was lying in the crook of my arm.

Teddy! Gone again! Boy, did I jump out of that corner seat!

Oh, no, he was on the floor.

He sat with his legs spread wide apart, rolling a tractor wheel around and around, while the boy— yes, Peik, that was his name—played with a "tay-shun" under the window and loaded plastic boxes onto a truck. The table had been folded down to make room for the station.

His sister was sitting where Teddy had been. She peered at me shyly under the long strands of hair that had escaped her braids.

Mrs. Breden chuckled at my bewildered face. She'd moved into the opposite corner to leave space for my legs.

"I—I don't usually sleep like this during the day. I can't understand it. You'd think I'd been given a sleeping pill."

"Oh, you obviously read detective stories. I don't think it's strange that you dozed off. The hum of the train always makes people sleepy. And maybe you had a lot to do before you left."

"Um." Anyone would think she knew!

"Peik gave you the teddy bear when he saw you were asleep. Your brother didn't need it any more. He didn't sleep very long."

I could well imagine. Teddy's never sleepy during the day and he doesn't sleep very much at night.

"He sat up almost immediately, but we've been playing and chattering while you rested."

Playing and chattering? Teddy? Was Mrs. Breden trying to make a fool out of me?

"I think he's clever." She bent forward. "Isn't that right, Teddy? Aren't you clever?"

"Teddy cl-lever." He said it to the tractor wheel and went on whirling it.

"Do you—do you really think he's clever?"

"Yes, indeed." Mrs. Breden wrinkled her forehead. "I just said so to Bente, didn't I?" A nod, which made her braids jump, came from Bente's direction.

"Teddy is cleverer than Peik in many ways, although Teddy's younger."

Younger! That was a pretty stupid joke, I thought. How could you call a big, heavy fifteen-year-old younger than a toddler?

Mrs. Breden straightened herself and drew closer to me. "Don't you understand what I mean? You should count Teddy's age from the moment the injury stopped his brain from developing. Right?"

"Injury? But he hasn't injured himself. Not that I know, at any rate."

"Perhaps. But there's a cause for everything. Agreed? Teddy wouldn't be . . . Teddy, if something hadn't happened to him at some point, something that kept him back, while other children developed."

"Yes, but I think he was born that way. Something was missing. . . ." I explained as well as I could about the part in his machinery. "That's how I've figured it."

But she didn't seem to think much of my explanation. "Well, perhaps, Mikkel. But *why* do you think that part is missing? Because the machinery has been damaged. And that might have happened before he was born. Often it's very difficult to determine just when it happened."

This was all very strange. But I liked it!

"Do you mean that it's just as if he'd hurt himself or been run over or something?"

"His injury may have been caused by pressure or a blow on the head, but it also might have been caused by a disease that changed something in his brain. There are so many different kinds of brain injury. I've worked for three years in a home for mentally defective children—"

"Are you a doctor?"

"No, a nurse. And I promise you that I've nursed children who are much worse off than Teddy."

"Oh." I was so stunned that I couldn't think of a thing to say.

Then Teddy simply had something the matter with him. Mother and Father hadn't been making it up when they said he was ill. Then there wasn't anything to be ashamed of. Nope. Not at all.

I could have hugged Mrs. Breden, I was so happy.

But she went on: "Now look at my Peik." She ruffled his hair. "He's two years and four months old. Teddy is probably slightly younger than he is—well, you understand now that I mean mentally, don't you?"

"Yes, sure."

"That's why Teddy is called mentally defective."

Yes. For the first time the words didn't sound ugly. Defective. A lot of people had defects. Teddy had a defective brain. Nothing wrong with that—it could have happened to anybody, even the plum girls, the sour woman, the Biters.

Biters. Chills ran up my spine.

It was one thing if someone had an injury, but that didn't mean he should injure other people.

It took a while before I could follow what Mrs. Breden was saying again. A bloody face hung in the air between us. But little by little she talked right around the face.

She went on comparing Peik and Teddy—how they talked and ate, to what extent they could dress themselves. Teddy led, she decided. "Actually, it's not a good idea to compare healthy people with people who are sick—it's never quite fair. But Teddy is surprising in a lot of ways. While you were sleeping, he drank juice from a mug without spilling a drop."

"It must have been a fluke."

"And he gets some kind of education, doesn't he?"

"No."

"Really? But he knows the names of a couple of letters. He pointed to my newspaper and said, 'A' and 'O.' "

"Was he right?"

"Er—no, he pointed to the wrong letters. But the very fact that he connects certain sounds with the figures in the paper is promising. How has he learned to do that?"

So I had to tell her that from time to time I tried to teach him, just for fun.

Oh, how eager she became! She almost sat down on top of me, and she fired off a series of questions about his "education."

I'd never thought anyone would take Teddy's

education seriously. Father always looks uneasy when we discuss it, and Mother's a bit out of it because of her Danish, even though she's glad we have something to occupy us.

"Can he really learn to correct his pronunciation?" It must have been the second time that Mrs. Breden had asked me.

"Not all the time. And I have to repeat every word over and over before he gets it."

"Yes, of course, that's natural."

Natural! My foot.

But I forgave her for not understanding what a struggle it was. She looked so darn funny squatting in front of Teddy and trying all sorts of tricks to "talk" with him.

She went on trying until Peik got angry and threw his whole station against the wall with a clatter. He sulked, pushed his mother away from Teddy, and after she returned to her seat, lay down across her knees and sucked his thumb.

"There, there, Peik." She took him in her arms and played ride a cock horse. "He seems so gentle too," she added after Peik had calmed down.

"Peik?"

"No, Teddy. He didn't protest because Peik took his teddy bear and played with it."

"He *is* good. He's never . . ." I got stuck again. Yesterday it would have been true. Not today.

Bente, who was following everything we said, looked as if she were waiting for me to continue. Not her mother, though.

"That's why it's so easy to become fond of these children. Most of them are so sweet. And it's thrilling to be with them. It's like rummaging in a chest full of old bits and pieces."

"Huh?"

"Yes, oddments. You may not find the piece you're looking for, but suddenly you come across the most beautiful piece of silk in the most wonderful colors. Something you never knew was there."

Just then Teddy belched.

"Shush, Teddy." Beautiful piece of silk, indeed! Bente covered her mouth, shocked. But Mrs. Breden didn't seem to mind. She simply nodded.

"Yes, that's one of the difficulties. Children like Teddy have no idea that there are some things they must do and some they mustn't because it isn't done or isn't nice or correct. They don't have any of the inhibitions that the rest of us walk around with. That's why we have to take good care of them, because they have to meet other people besides us— isn't that true? So it's our responsibility to see that they don't break the law or annoy other people in any way."

That shot went home!

I hadn't been able to handle that responsibility.

6

Another Ball Game

"Trains don't make you feel sick, do they, Mikkel?"

"I beg your pardon? Oh, no." I quickly screwed my face into a smile. It would be safer to wear a mask and follow the lecture.

She went on telling me all about her "children"— what they said and did. No wonder she knew so much about Teddy. Mother and Father hadn't worked for years in hospitals or children's homes.

Mrs. Breden wasn't ashamed of laughing when Teddy curled up to suck his finger like Peik but didn't find a finger that suited him. He tasted one after the other—all ten, I think—but just turned up his nose at them.

"Don't they taste good, Teddy? Would you rather eat a cookie?" She handed him one with a smile.

"There you are, Peik. The boy thinks you should

eat something real." Lisping Bente was not told to stop laughing. It was all right to have fun with Teddy—there was nothing wrong with it.

It was good to realize that so many of the things I'd felt inside me were correct. But it would have been wonderful to have a clear conscience too— nothing to worry about or be afraid of.

I guess Mrs. Breden was something of a mind reader, because she asked me where we were going to stay in Malberg.

"We're—we're going to my uncle's cottage," I stuttered.

"I suppose he'll meet you at the station?"

The compartment was beginning to get hot.

"Er—no. He can't." That way she might think he was planning to send someone else.

I turned to Teddy and scolded him to avoid more questions. "You mustn't take the truck away from Peik."

But Peik had fallen asleep, and Mrs. Breden's questions continued. She didn't pry, but she was obviously interested.

"Is this your vacation, then, that you're spending with your uncle?"

"Vacation? No. Yes. This is our fall vacation." I'd almost forgotten that it was. Mrs. Breden was getting difficult. I began to wish that we'd stayed in the other compartment after all.

"A vacation already?" She put Peik carefully down on the seat and spread the jacket, which had served as a pillow for Teddy and me, over the boy.

"You'll just stay with him a couple of days, I suppose?"

I could have done with a recipe for an answer that was neither Yes nor No. Now I pretended to be completely absorbed in the view.

It didn't stop her, though. She drew in breath for the next round. I rose and looked out of the window.

"I can see the mountains."

"Yes, the hills are getting higher." The danger was over for the time being. She told me that she and the children were going to spend a week's vacation in a boarding house. They'd had bad luck during the summer: all three of them had caught measles, she too, "although I had them as a child."

Then Peik had come down with an ear infection. Bente hadn't been well, either. "Have you had the measles?"

"No." But I was very grateful that she'd had them. I examined her for as long as I could about fever and red spots; I tried to appear fascinated by red throats and red eyes.

Finally Mrs. Breden asked, "Are you afraid of catching them? Is there an epidemic of measles in the neighborhood where you live or something?"

"No, I don't think so. But it's always a good idea to know a little bit about—"

"Yes, of course. And you ought to be on the lookout. If Teddy caught the measles he'd probably get very sick."

Thank you. That was a great ball she'd served me. Now I had a new set of questions to fire at her.

But then the train braked. It squeaked and yammered before it resigned itself and stood still at the station. Peik woke up again, but he squalled more than the train did and had to be cuddled.

Good boy, Peik! Everybody fussed over him.

Teddy sat with the truck in his lap, looking lost.

" 'Ave it. Is miiiine," Peik whined. He managed to tear it away. Teddy didn't try to stop him, but he bent forward to retrieve it—and that was lucky. For at that moment, the wall behind him disappeared. An old man pushed open the door that Teddy had been leaning against.

"Are there any seats in here?" he spurted through his chewing tobacco.

"Yes, do sit down," Mrs. Breden answered. We tidied up the kindergarten and moved Teddy into a corner.

I was glad that someone else had joined us. I was grateful for anything that might distract Mrs. Breden from thinking about our destination and whom we were going to visit.

The man sank down beside Bente, and the two of them smiled toothlessly at each other.

He put his knobbly stick between his knees and plunked a funny kind of satchel on top of them.

After that he didn't provide any more entertainment. Now it was his turn to study us. Small slanted eyes moved inside the cracks in his wrinkles, but the head itself didn't turn.

"Goodness. Has so much time passed already? Are you going far from Malberg Station?"

We were off again—both the train and Mrs. Breden.

"Oh, yes, quite far. Look! Peik wants to play with Teddy."

"So he does. The boy can't stack those boxes, Peik. You'll have to do that yourself. Will you be met by car?"

"Car? N-n-nooo, that won't be necessary. Peik seems to want to sit on his lap," I added, looking at the old man.

"Careful, you kicked him. I'm so sorry. Why don't you sit with me, Peik, and let the boy borrow your tractor? Can't you see that he wants to turn the wheels? Then the cottage isn't at the top of the mountain."

I had a terrible coughing fit. But it wasn't the cough that made my back and the palms of my hands perspire.

"Here. Drink a little juice." The red plastic mug was held in front of me.

I couldn't cough myself out of everything she wanted to know. Mrs. Breden got far too many dangerous shots at the goal. And I got quite exhausted from throwing myself around trying to guard it. No matter where I threw the ball, she maneuvered herself into a position to throw it back.

I'd never played a harder game.

"Thank you very much. I sound as if I had whooping cough."

A miss. Whooping cough didn't go over as well as the measles.

She took the mug again and looked earnestly at me. A searching look is what they call it. Oh, don't look at me like that. I knew she knew the cough wasn't genuine. And I felt ashamed.

The conductor came in and took the old man's ticket. He'd kept it behind his ear.

"So you can keep more than foxes behind your ear, then." That shot was aimed at me. Mrs. Breden asked the conductor how soon we would reach Malberg.

"In three quarters of an hour. We're running on time."

Forty-five minutes! Even in the dentist's chair time goes more quickly than it did on the train. The long hours we'd spent in the morning seemed like minutes now.

Peik was a gem. He wanted "potty." And out to the washroom he trooped with Mrs. Breden and Bente. What a break!

I used it to think up some topics of conversations. I couldn't afford any pauses. She might sneak in a shot. She was already suspicious, but if she realized that we were completely on our own, she would get off the train at Malberg, children and all, and see us right to Uncle's cottage. Not a soul there? Straight to the nearest telephone. The nearest . . .

For the first time I remembered how far it was from the village to the cottage. Up, up, up all those hills and then across. . . . How would we ever manage it tonight?

It got dark much earlier now than during the

summer. I'd forgotten that. Where were my brains? Should I listen to the danger signals buzzing in my head and go home? "It's our responsibility to see that they don't break the law or annoy other people in any way. . . ." Teddy had broken the law, and I had to take the consequences—I could take them. It didn't matter if they locked me up. Well, it mattered a little. But they were after Teddy, and he didn't deserve to be punished.

My break lasted eight minutes.

Mrs. Breden and her children returned and talked among themselves, so I couldn't launch myself on my thrilling conversational program of "Do you think the weather will be as fine tomorrow as it is today?" or "Why is that river so green?" or "Living on the shady side of the valley must get very tiresome."

"Yes, don't you think so?" asked Mrs. Breden above me.

"Sure."

From Bente's giggles and expression I understood that the question had been directed at her, not me.

"You seem to have a lot to think about, Mikkel." Mrs. Breden was pulling my leg. She sat down.

"Not an awful lot. This side—side of the valley is in shadow already."

"Is that where you're going? Or does your uncle live on the sunny side?"

Help! "Er—I don't know."

"You don't? Don't you know Malberg?"

"Oh, yes. Yes, indeed. But we haven't arrived yet.

Maybe the sun shines differently there. . . ." No, I was making no sense. I didn't dare stay in the compartment a minute longer.

"Could you look after Teddy for a moment, please?"

A good move. Teddy didn't even look after me as I closed the door. He'd really been clever and quiet during the last couple of hours.

Clever . . . To think that he *was* clever. That it wasn't just something we said to cheer him up.

I stood at the end of the corridor and tried to recognize the mountains by their shapes. I heard a time signal from the troublemakers' compartment: they had a transistor radio. After the time signal, news about the weather is broadcast, and after that comes the news and then the police messages.

I had to wait—had to know if the police were looking for Bjarne and Mikael Grabseth!

I'd have to spend the last fifteen minutes listening. Mrs. Breden would probably think there was a line waiting to get into the washroom. Anyway, it didn't matter what she believed, as long as she stayed where she was.

I stole past our compartment door and tried it carefully. Yes, it was shut. She wouldn't be able to hear the radio through a crack.

There was room for me beside a—hah—beside the magazine girl. She was leaning on the window across from the troublemakers' open door, with a silk scarf over her head that fluttered.

She probably wasn't interested in the weather

81

forecast, but I didn't think she'd manage to get acquainted with the gang. Their mood seemed rather sour. They were half asleep or chatting, their eyes bleak. Cigarettes dangled at chin level.

"End of weather forecast." I listened through several newspaper pages of politics, then a report about an airplane that had had to make an emergency landing, a fire in a factory, sportscast . . . and police messages.

"We have a police message from Hordaland police station"—that couldn't be us. No—"An elderly lady is missing." Not a word about two boys.

We had a good start. But I'd have given a lot to know what was happening. If the police met someone who could put them on our trail . . . well, it was inevitable, sooner or later.

"I just told Bente to go and look for you. We're almost there. You'd better get your things together."

Mrs. Breden lifted the rucksack down for me and said "Excuse me" again to the old man, this time because he was sitting on the teddy bear's leg.

"Are you getting off now?" He edged himself forward and handed me the bear.

"Yes. Thank you." Into the rucksack with it, and out with Teddy's sweater.

"I can see the green light of Malberg Station up ahead," said Mrs. Breden. "How long will it take you to get from the station to—didn't you say Solhelle?"

"No, Vingomli." Help! I'd fallen into the trap again. Headlong.

"But Vingomli is right at the top. How are you going to get there if you're not being met by car?"

Sorry. I was so busy rummaging in the rucksack that I didn't hear Mrs. Breden.

The old man showed the yellow stumps at the back of his mouth and thanked us for our company when I led Teddy out of the compartment. Mrs. Breden followed me, her two children in tow.

Teddy's fist was tightly squeezed in mine. The train never waited long at small stations, and it was already slowing down.

DANGER. DO NOT LEAN OUT said the sign under the window, but at least half of Mrs. Breden was outside as we puffed toward the gray building and the people on the platform.

"What does your uncle look like?"

She must have forgotten that I'd told her he wasn't going to meet us.

"Big and tall with light brown hair like Teddy's. Yes, he's like Teddy, or rather Teddy's like him. Teddy is called Bjarne after Uncle Bjarne. . . ."

I talked as if I were an express train, while the train itself chugged more and more slowly. A couple of seconds, and I would be spared any further questions.

"I don't see anyone who—" Mrs. Breden pulled in her head and rubbed her eye—"who looks like Teddy. Oh!" She got a black stripe on her cheek from rubbing it, but she couldn't get the soot out of her eye.

"He probably hasn't come *himself*, then. Thank

you very much for your company and all your help.
Come along, Teddy."

The door was open, but Teddy stopped when he
saw the steps. He didn't want to climb down.
"You've got to come, Teddy. Be clever."

But he clutched the doorpost, not daring to take
the last big step down to the platform.

"You jump down, Mikkel, and hold him." Mrs.
Breden certainly managed things. She soothed him,
loosened his grip, put her arm around his shoulders,
and helped him down. Step by step.

I could never have done it without her. "Thanks."

Peik wanted to jump down too, and while she
scooped him up, I maneuvered Teddy a few steps
away. "Good-bye. Enjoy the rest of your trip." I
waved when I heard the conductor call, "Take your
seats."

She seemed frightened and worried as she looked
down the platform and back at us. She kept rubbing
her eye, and the smudge of soot on her cheek grew
larger.

"But I can't leave you. Don't you see anybody
you know here?"

"Oh, yes, of course." I turned around and waved
at some people near the newspaper stand who were
gazing at the traffic. I don't know whether she swallowed that one. Now the train began to move, and
the stationmaster, or whoever it was, ran over and
closed the door in front of her and the children.

A black, smudged cheek and a blinking eye
against the glass pane, and then they were gone.

I stood there feeling like a crook.

A fine way to thank kind people who only wanted to help. Lie and cheat and run away and make her get soot in her eye from looking for Uncle Bjarne.

I spat on the platform angrily. The men next to the stand shook their heads. They must have thought it was a strange boy who first waved and smiled and then spat at them.

On the hill behind the fence there were a couple of sheep. I pointed them out to Teddy and discussed the merits of Norwegian wool as compared to Shetland wool. (I'd recently seen a program about the Shetland Islands on Leif Arne's television.)

It was all the same to Teddy—he didn't care. But the men turned as one man and looked at the sheep instead of us as we walked past them and around the corner of the building. Baaaa.

On a ramp behind the station the porter was busy piling cartons, which someone inside was handing him. Both men were too busy to notice us.

Now we had to do a fade-out, so no one would be able to tell where we'd gone. But how could we disappear from a station that only boasted a large wooden building, a small one, and a newspaper stand? There was a kind of shed a little further down the railroad tracks, but we couldn't play cowboys and Indians and crawl through the grass to it. Not Teddy.

Some kind of signal rang in the station, and the porter strode across the cartons, back to the office. On his way he informed his companion that he'd better find that freight bill. "Or he'll be down on us like a ton of bricks, buddy."

A heavy sigh and the rustling of paper could be heard behind the boards.

This was our chance! "Come on, let's go."

We drifted along the path by the tracks, and I pretended to be a tourist. I cocked my head and admired the mountains, gazed with interest at some telegraph poles that were strewn over a nearby slope. At the same time I peered over my shoulder, because I had to know what was happening.

The porter and his friend were still inside, and the few people walking on the road all had their backs turned to us.

Teddy trotted along happily; he probably enjoyed walking after sitting still for so long.

Now we were near the shed. Only a couple of steps more, a last quick glance—I didn't see a soul —and we were sheltered. In three directions, any-way—there was no wall on the side facing the tracks.

Crates—the kind with bars for dogs and some ordinary ones—were stacked in the shed. A trolley and an old sledge leaned against a wall. There was a little pile of wood shavings and splinters in one corner.

"We can stay here till it's dark, Teddy. If nobody comes, ha ha."

Soon it would get dark. The hills in front of us and behind us were already in shadow. A fiery red haze above the ridge of one hill was our only reminder of the sun.

"Later on we'll sneak through the village without anybody seeing us." I laughed and Teddy joined in with chuckles.

We sat on one of the boxes, and although there wasn't anything funny about our situation, I couldn't stop my crazy laughter. It kept bubbling in my throat.

"Do you see how thick the forest is on that hill, hee hee hee? Once we get up there, it won't be easy to find us, ho ho ho. We're going straight up there, across that black ridge, hee hee ho ho."

Teddy faithfully joined in with my fits of laughter.

"Shush, we mustn't laugh, someone might hear us, oh hee hee hee! Do you know that it usually takes about three hours to get up to the cottage? Eeh-hee—"

Suddenly I realized that my laughter was just as false as my coughing fit on the train. What I really wanted to do was cry. I wanted to give in and howl.

I couldn't bear to think how long Teddy and I would have to trudge in the dark before we reached the cottage.

7

Shelter

"Mi-ine, this." It was Teddy's voice, but the sulky inflection was Peik's.

I lifted my head, and sure enough, Teddy was kneeling in the sawdust, playing cars with a wooden stick.

No, he wasn't using a piece of wood from the shed. He had a small toy car in his hand. "That must be Peik's car. You took it."

"Teddy cl-lever." He smiled and chuckled gaily across the planks.

So now we were stealing. Mrs. Breden would probably understand it wasn't intentional. I should have thought of searching through his pockets for toys. But maybe he'd held the car in his left hand all the time.

There was nothing else in his pockets, except the old crust of bread, and I threw that to the birds.

Come to think of it, it might be a good idea to eat something before we started the long uphill walk, while we could still see what we put into our mouths.

I dished up the food as well as I could on a crate, cut the bread and buttered a couple of slabs for each of us. We sat down and watched the lights go on in one window after another across the river. There were more houses over there than on the station side. We would need luck to sneak past them.

"It's no use getting jittery in advance or making plans," I explained to Teddy. "We'll have to take things as they come."

The food tasted of train soot and tar, because that's what the shed smelled of. And herring! I'm sure there was an empty herring barrel lurking in the dark somewhere.

I'd heard the noise of shutters and doors being closed in the station, but now everything was quiet.

I ventured to put my nose out a few inches and saw two figures under the light in front of the station. One of them walked to the little building and tried the doors; then he jogged to catch up with his friend. The station must have closed for the day.

But what would they do now? Were they pushing or lifting something across the road? I couldn't see a thing, but it sounded as if they were closing a gate.

Maybe they'd locked it, and we wouldn't be able to leave the station. But we had to. At once.

Brrr, how cold we were. I shook myself and rubbed Teddy's back, but he didn't like it. He grunted angrily and commanded, "Go home!"

I couldn't make out whether he meant that I should go away or that it was time for both of us to go home.

"Yes, we're going, Teddy. Now stand up so I can put your parka on you."

We fumbled with the hood and arms but finally got it on.

"Come on—no, careful." Teddy stumbled and nearly fell over the rucksack. I'd forgotten all about it! It would have been a fine thing if we'd walked away without our "luggage."

We might need the flashlight, but I didn't want to turn it on here. In the forest I'd take a chance and use it.

Little clusters of starry lights shone on both hills, so we knew where the farms were. The bridge was well lit, and the road that we were going to take was visible a good way up the hill. But farther up, there was just black and more black.

On the other side of the river we'd have to cross the highway, where there was lots of traffic. The headlights of cars driving south illumined the whole road, from bend to bend. I didn't like the cars driving north. I couldn't see where they were going.

Now we had to be careful. The road behind the main building was the only one leading out of the station.

"Be quiet, Teddy," I whispered in his ear. "Quiet. Shush."

"A'noon nap," he answered, and then he didn't make a sound. Yes, he *was* clever. We'd taught him at home to be as quiet as a mouse while Father was taking his afternoon nap. Usually Teddy forgets after a few minutes, but this time he didn't.

No one came out to see who was skulking around the main building, even though a lamp shone behind lace curtains on the first floor, making everything red.

That must be where the stationmaster lived. He was probably the guy who'd come down like a ton of bricks on the man who couldn't find the freight bill.

I walked faster and almost lost my arm trying to get Teddy quickly past the house of the bogeyman.

I found a gate, and it didn't have a lock—just a hook. I lifted it and pushed the gate very carefully so it wouldn't make any noise, but it squawked and whined, and I had to stop.

"Squeeze through here, Teddy."

Because I was still whispering, he paid me back with a loud hissing "Sssshusssh!" And—squeeze? He walked smack into the middle of the gate. The hook jumped out of my fingers, and the whole gate slammed into the ditch on the other side with a noise that would have put most train whistles to shame!

Ohhh! I held my breath. . . . Sure enough, they'd heard us. The station suddenly came to life.

The door on the platform opened, and a tall man ran out—a big, strong man.

Down. Down. Now I didn't even whisper, I just thought the words, and pulled Teddy down beside me in the ditch. We lay on our faces.

The man in front of the house seemed to turn toward us.

(Lie still, Teddy. Lie still!)

No, I guess he didn't see us against the dark hill. He jumped down on the tracks and disappeared. I heard the click of metal; he must be changing the switches. A moment later the tracks began to hum. The signal lights turned from green to red along the line. Another train was arriving.

Teddy and I sat, our chins between our knees, watching it as it thundered into Malberg. The gate closed behind us; I'd been able to hook it again during all the noise.

The train didn't stop. The lighted compartments flew past us like a film strip. I thought that people inside must be warm and comfortable. I wondered if anyone looking out of the train could see us.

Durr dang, durr dang, durr dang. The last carriage rattled over the switches, and I immediately went into high gear.

As long as the lighted train wound its way through the valley, no one would notice a couple of boys walking along the road, past the schoolhouse and the shop, across the square in front of the cafe— fortunately, there were no faces in the windows— and trudging toward the bridge.

We had to pass three more houses on our side of the river.

Houses number one and two were quiet, but something was happening in the garage of number three. A Volkswagen was backed halfway into it, and under a dangling light bulb a man stood cutting shiny wires with a pair of clippers.

I couldn't make up my mind whether we should walk past him or not. The light from the gatepost lamps was pretty strong.

"Daddy," Teddy called and tried to run to the man. I braked so hard that a shingle crunched underneath me, and held on to him firmly.

"No, that isn't Father's car." I said it loudly and clearly because the man came to the door of the garage and peered out. Fortunately we were standing behind a bush.

"Father's picking us up in the Volvo," I continued to broadcast. I didn't want the man to think we were aiming for the hill.

But he didn't seem to think anything. He was already immersed in his wires and connections again and obviously didn't care who was walking in the light of his gatepost lamps.

Even so, I turned several times before we reached the bridge, just to make sure he wasn't following us.

I wondered how Teddy would react to crossing the river. Would he be frightened by all the water streaming below us? Didn't he hear the sloshing of the river and the whoosh of the wind?

No, he didn't. He was completely lost in himself, and walked along mumbling. It sounded as though he said, "Daddy" a couple of times. He probably thought we were going to wind up in front of our own gate, after all.

Typical! We would have to meet a shaky cyclist

on the middle of the bridge. Well, there was plenty of room, but too much light and no bushes. There was nothing we could do but walk on. We certainly couldn't jump into the river!

But the cyclist must have had his mind on other things. He barely glanced at us.

It was only a short distance to the crossroads by the highway on the other side of the bridge. We had to walk across the highway and bear right to the bend. I remembered the road so well that I didn't have to look at the sign.

The highway wasn't exactly a one-lane affair, and an enormous trailer thundered past us before we crossed the road. The trailer was so heavy that the earth trembled, and Teddy said, "Doon, doon" in his roughest voice.

Luckily he stopped it before we reached a group of cooperative houses. A handful of boys and girls were hanging around outside. We stayed on the other side of the road and stared straight ahead as we passed them.

They looked at us. They were suddenly quiet, and the silence followed us pace by pace. They were watching us closely, and that was dangerous.

If only I'd had an invisible leash for Teddy. They obviously couldn't understand why Teddy and I were walking hand in hand.

At least they didn't yell anything nasty at us. Maybe teenagers are a little kinder in the country. . . .

It's hard to see in the dark when the road winds

uphill. Lifting my legs got tougher and tougher, and Teddy lagged behind me all the time. The real climb still lay ahead of us. I remembered that Father usually shifted into second gear about now. The road wound toward the forest in endless hairpin curves, which made it look even longer.

"We'd better go this way, Teddy." There was a footpath that cut across the curves through the fields.

Phew, it was steep.

Teddy hadn't taken more than a few steps on our first short cut before he announced, "No!" and turned down the hill again. We had to rest a little. I couldn't see anything to sit on, so we just leaned against a fence.

It wasn't exactly the coziest place to rest.

The air had gotten so cold that everything we put our hands on felt clammy. I didn't mind the rich smell of manure, but the darkness was horrid. There weren't many lights on the roads up in the hills, and we were off the road, anyway, so we could hardly expect to see very much.

Oh! I started and ducked as something fluttered by my feet and flew over our heads. It was probably a crow, but it didn't caw.

We heard a noise on one of the neighboring farms. A dog barked, and then it was Teddy's turn to jump in the air. Suppose the dog were loose and came bounding toward us!

"You're right, Teddy; it's too steep here. Too dark. We'd be better off taking the road. Come on."

He followed me as long as I chattered, and we

didn't hear the dog again. Slowly, slowly, we worked our way up the hill toward a cluster of houses with lighted windows.

We finally struggled around and above the cluster and saw another group of houses smiling at us with their lights up to the left.

But I hardly dared look beyond them and to our right and over the rest of the hillside. For there darkness spread itself, a darkness so dark that it didn't make any difference if I closed my eyes.

There was the forest. The night.

"Go home now."

Well, we'd have to stop again.

"Look down the hill, Teddy. Look at all the dots of light down there. Look at the car—see, it's moving. See that stripe?"

I made an effort and pointed, but Teddy didn't pay any attention.

"Go home!" Again. Oh, if only we could.

"We've got to walk a little more. Just a little."

I heard the sound of cart wheels and the trampling of hoofs somewhere above us on the hill. We'd have to get off the road because Teddy is frightened of horses. And horses are frightened of him. I'd noticed that many times.

But where could we hide? Behind the stone wall along the road? It was high enough to hide us, but I wanted to get farther away. In the grove of trees? I caught a glimpse of something that looked like a little tumbledown shack. We'd better struggle over to it.

"Come on, let's climb over the stones, Teddy. Like this!"

Not a good suggestion. Teddy wasn't in the mood to pretend he was a weasel, nor was he in training. I gave up trying to drag him across the stones.

We'd have to run to the end of the wall, but would we have time? The horse was already on the curve above us; its light body was visible for a moment among the bushes.

I don't know if Teddy saw it, but of course he must have heard the hoofbeats. He got restless.

"Yes, the horse is coming. Dangerous. Run fast!"

It was mean to scare him, but I didn't know how else to make him hurry. He clung to me with both hands and squeaked, "No-oh."

I ran, and because he didn't dare let go, he staggered after me. When he's frightened, he always walks very clumsily and stiffly, stepping on air most of the time.

We reached the end of the wall just before the horse swung around the last curve. It was a good thing, because otherwise the horse would have come straight at us, and goodness knows what would have happened.

We bumped and hobbled and stumbled over tufts of grass. I didn't need to say a word about the horse to Teddy; he heard it snorting behind us and was terrified.

"Huh, huh, huh." His breathing sounded like a steam engine as we tumbled into the little shack— "tumbled" because the opening was high in the wall.

There was no door, and there didn't seem to be much floor. Half the roof had fallen in, and we sat on the rotten rafters that were scattered around. But I patted the moss-covered timber, because the shack was our friend. And a weak wall was a hundred times better than no wall between us and the horse.

The horse slowed down just before it reached the fence and bunched its legs together to withstand the pressure of the shafts. It obviously sensed us, but the man sitting on a sack in the back of the cart didn't. He just tugged at the reins, clicked, and tried to coax the horse: "Hup! Hup! Git on, Blakka!"

Blakka tossed her head and rattled the harness. But then she blew a long *prrrrrro* toward us and rumbled on downhill.

I don't know if Teddy meant to imitate Blakka or whether he was just sighing with relief. At any rate, he blew right into my ear after the horse and cart had disappeared from the circle of light under the lamppost.

"Now it isn't dangerous." Perhaps I shouldn't have told him that, because I probably wouldn't be able to make him hurry without scaring him. He wasn't a bit interested in going anywhere.

But we couldn't stay long in the raw, cold, miserable air. I felt a little ashamed that I wasn't more grateful to the poor, tumbledown shed.

I decided to turn on the flashlight and investigate the shack. It mightn't be as bad as it seemed. Oh, yes. Ugh! Even when I held my hand in front of the flashlight and flashed it quickly, I saw enough sheep droppings, cobwebs, fungus, and slimy, rotten grass to think twice about lying down.

"You're a little too unprotected to use as a night shelter, pal. But thanks for your help. We won't forget you." I gave the turf on the roof a last pat as I climbed out, and then I left both the shack and Teddy. I wondered what he would do.

First I heard some protesting and grumbling noises. Then he stumbled over the high threshold, exactly as he had when we'd entered.

"El-lik."

"Here I am." I waited in the bushes.

And would you believe it? He came!

Was it really all that simple? Could I just walk on ahead? I glanced back from time to time. Yes, he'd gotten up and was following me.

"Come home now," he wheedled sweetly in Mother's voice. But I pretended not to hear him and walked on.

The farm we were about to pass seemed to be the last in the neighborhood. The lampposts ended where the farm road diverged from the hairpin curves. We'd have to make do with a flashlight and cats' eyes.

It wasn't that I was afraid of the dark. I wasn't afraid of the forest, either. But there's quite a difference between a forest during the day and a forest at night.

To make matters worse, Teddy started to fall behind again. Was it from weariness or because he didn't like the dark? Both, probably.

I knew it was our bedtime. And I also got very chilly waiting for him at every little slope and bend. My hands were cold, even though I'd put them in my pockets.

"Come on, Teddy. Hurry up." I tried to speak naturally, the way we do when lunch is ready.

"Blah, stupid!" He was scolding himself somewhere below me. "Stupid, stupid." The children at home used to call him that.

He stumbled again. I'd have to lead him. We'd get nowhere like this.

But when I stooped and helped him to his feet, he refused to budge. "Go home," he demanded again. " 'T once!" At once. Now he was angry.

What should I do?

I knew we couldn't reach the cottage tonight, and we had to get under a roof. It was far too cold to sleep in the forest without sleeping bags.

I'm not sure I'd have slept in the forest *with* a sleeping bag. The trees made such eerie noises. Bears —suppose a real live bear were rooting in the forest.

Give up, Mikkel. You may as well give up.

Had I heard the words, or had I just thought them? You get so muddled when you're tired.

"Home *now*."

"Okay, okay. Come on, then." I took Teddy by the hand, and we slunk toward the farm. That's how I felt, giving up, throwing in the sponge. I should have had a white flag to enter enemy territory.

Not that the light beaming from the windows was unfriendly. On the contrary. But how could I tell what kind of people lived in the house? What did they know? Yes, there were telephone lines. And they'd have a radio, of course.

The time was eight minutes past ten. The evening news would be broadcast any minute.

A large barn shadowed the other buildings, although it was a whole story lower than the road. You could only get to the hayloft from our side over a bridge of wooden planks. The doors on the ground story probably led to the stables and pigsties. That's what it smelled like, anyway.

Grunting, a kick against the side of a stall, and a moo so sleepy that it turned into a *mmmmmmmm* proved my nose to be right.

I peered around the corner of the barn, down at the three buildings that enclosed a yard. A little snow sprinkled here and there and the farm would have looked like a Chirtsmas card. I couldn't make up my mind. What should I do? Go down to the big house, knock on the big double doors and say, "Excuse me, may we spend the night here?"

"Look out, get back, Teddy!" Someone had banged one of the windows shut in the big house and turned out the light. Two of the Christmas card squares were covered up.

They seemed to be going to bed. They'd be annoyed if we disturbed them now. I wasn't so sure they'd let us in, either, if they took a close look at Teddy.

We might as well have tacked labels saying RUN-AWAY FROM HOME on us. At any rate, if we asked for shelter for the night, the telephone wires down the valley would start humming. If I owned the farm and two boys like us asked to spend the night, I'd phone to find out whether they'd been reported missing.

And there would be phone calls to our home, conferences about returning us, fetching us. . . . Help! Teddy was teetering on the planks that went up to the hayloft. "Don't move."

I jumped up, grabbed his arm, and dragged him down to me. A step or two more and he would have walked over the edge. He didn't realize that there was nothing underneath the planks. He didn't know it was possible to fall so far. He probably wanted to go into the building to get warm.

Into—into the barn!

"Teddy," I whispered. "You're clever. Very clever."

Why hadn't I thought of the barn before? We were standing on the threshold of a perfect shelter. All we had to do was lift the latch and walk in.

I don't think anyone heard us, because we didn't exactly tramp across the bridge. It was littered with hay and straw, which muffled our footsteps. The door squeaked a little on its hinges but not very much.

"Huh heh." Teddy also smelled the hay—how strange. He doesn't usually smell things, but he could obviously sense the strong, sweet air that enveloped us.

He wanted to leave the moment we got inside, however, so I couldn't close the door behind us.

"Put on light."

"Don't be afraid, I'm looking after you. It isn't dangerous."

He wasn't reassured. He still wanted to get out. At home we leave his bedside lamp on all night. I'd have to turn on the flashlight and hope the walls had no chinks. I wouldn't want the people in the house to get suspicious.

I found the flashlight in the rucksack. Actually, we needed a bit of light. Tractor equipment and tools were strewn all over the place. If we'd bumped into the iron frame that was placed against a beam to our left we'd certainly have made a fine noise. Or suppose we'd stumbled on the teeth of the big hay rake!

I pulled Teddy away from all the dangerous objects and was delighted to see that halfway across the floor the flashlight shone on nothing but hay. Enormous, swelling mounds of soft, lovely, cozy hay.

"We can sleep here, Teddy. There, now, make yourself at home. Sit down."

He just stood there, so I swung around quickly and pulled him down with me. We fell on a huge, springy cushion of hay. It swayed and rocked with us. And we didn't sink in too far.

"Ha. Hahahahahee." This was fun. Teddy slapped his arms on the hay and bounced. We romped and rolled, but then I had to quiet him down.

To be on the safe side, I dug a little den for the

flashlight so it only gave out a faint light. We couldn't risk anybody noticing that there were uninvited guests in the barn. I giggled nervously. "Are you hungry, Teddy? Food?"

"Not dang'rous." He rocked in reply. I thought I could hear snickering and see the plum girls' eyes as I broke off a lump of bread.

He took it—he always does when we offer him food—but he just nibbled a little at the crust. I was too tired to eat.

I dragged Winnie-the-Pooh out and stuffed it in his arms, snatched some tufts of hay and patted them smooth.

"Now you have a blanket too. Go to sleep. Night night."

But Teddy whimpered and wriggled. "Take 'im away." The straws were stinging him.

The raincoats were at the bottom of the rucksack. Teddy seemed satisfied after I'd put one of them under him like a sheet—so satisfied that he started his usual evening concert.

"Na na na na," he sang on one note.

"Shush, not so loud." His singing makes my head reel, but I didn't dare put my fingers in my ears in case someone from the farm heard the racket.

Fortunately, the animals were stamping, lowing, and snorting down in the stables.

Teddy must have been terribly tired, because he'd agreed to lie down in the huge, strange, dark room without making a fuss.

But now I had to turn off the flashlight to save the

battery; I didn't have a spare one. Teddy stopped singing as soon as our cozy well-lighted den vanished.

I could make out a few objects, though, as some sort of light came in through two openings in the roof. If I'd seen the chinks before, I wouldn't have dared use the flashlight.

The raincoat rustled a lot when I burrowed into the hay. But no sound came from Teddy, so he must have fallen asleep. Poor Teddy. What a muddle I'd gotten him into in one—*one* day.

I had a bad conscience. Everything I was afraid of, dreaded, and worried about suddenly poured over me all at once. My chest felt tight, but my head floated. It was too small for all the thoughts that whirled around inside it.

Mother and Father—how were they? Not very well, I was sure. If only I could have talked to them without other people hearing us. The worst thing was that I hadn't managed the responsibility. If I'd looked after Teddy properly, we wouldn't be lying in a barn like outlaws.

I was terribly afraid, so small and despairing.

My eyelids and throat were sore.

Just then Teddy dug his head into my side and laid his arm across mine. "Look after you," he comforted—himself, probably, "Not dang'rous." And he was copying my voice!

He made me feel big and strong, after all.

I took his hand and promised to take good care of

my little brother. And suddenly I remembered what Mrs. Breden had told me about not always finding what you're looking for in the trunk but finding something unexpected and much lovelier instead.

8

Keep Going, Teddy

What a terrible drone!

Something was creeping over my nose. A spider? No, just a straw.

Ugh, I itched all over—inside my shirt, trousers, everywhere.

I felt clammy too. My clothes stuck to me. I shook my arms to sort of loosen them.

I brushed my blanket of hay off my clothes and rubbed dust out of my eyes and wondered what was droning below us. It wasn't a car or an airplane or a boat—it certainly wasn't a boat.

Several rays of light shone through trap doors in the roof on tools, hay and planks. There were a lot of openings, not just two as I'd thought. Teddy had kicked off the hay, so he was lying with nothing over him. His legs twitched from time to time.

Clank! came a noise through the drone of the

machine. And more rattling of buckets—they'd started milking the cows! The drone came from the milking machines, of course.

And there were people below us, although I'd meant to wake up at the crack of dawn. It was only quarter past six, but people get up much earlier in the country.

"Oooooh!" bellowed Teddy, half asleep. He often does that—he's our alarm clock at home—but maybe he was trying to mimic the sound of the milking machines.

"Sssshhhh, ssssshhhh. Wake up quietly, Teddy. Quietly?"

He opened his eyes when I touched his arm, looked past me, yawned, and called, "Mooothah."

No! This was dangerous. I held my hand over his mouth, but he twisted away and called Mother again.

"Get up, Teddy, get up." It took a while, but at least he tried. He kicked while I pulled, which only made him sink further into the hay. I had to help him roll over. That was better. Finally I managed to get him on his feet.

And none too soon; I was sure someone would find us any moment.

The loaf, the flashlight. I bundled them into the rucksack and strapped it on my shoulders.

Before I led Teddy outside, I pushed the big door ajar and squinted out. I saw two enormous pails in front of an open door far below us, but no one seemed to be around. We had to risk it.

"Look at the sky, how lovely and red it is," I whispered, so he wouldn't look at the planks. He followed my finger until we got across. What would I have done if he'd refused to walk over the bridge?

The farmyard was empty. Through the open stable door I could make out a cow's tail waving. If we could just walk away, we would be so lucky—oh!

A head suddenly popped up out of nowhere. A head with a green flowered scarf on it.

"Well, I thought there was someone in the loft."

A large girl with red cheeks and rolled-up shirt sleeves climbed up some narrow stairs beside the bridge. She must have been right beneath us.

"Er, well, yes . . ." I stuttered. She didn't look angry but surprised.

"Do you know the road to Vin—no, to Dalseter?" Dalseter was quite far away from Vingomli.

"Are you heading for Dalseter? Well, follow this road as far as that brown farm down there." She pointed down the road we'd trudged on the day before and explained a great deal I didn't listen to. After all, we weren't going in that direction.

Did she really believe we'd come to the farm at six in the morning to ask the way, or was she just being kind and pretending? We were so covered with hay, and our clothes were so crumpled and horrible that she must have guessed we'd slept in the barn. Especially if she'd heard us in the loft.

"You're up early." She put her hands under her

plastic apron and squinted in the sun. Or was she laughing at us? "But the weather's good."

"Yes, the weather's great. Yes, thank you very much," I said with a bow. Teddy was polite too. He nodded a bow and said, "Thank you, lovely meal." But I think I managed to cough away the meal.

"Have a good walk." The girl smiled knowingly as she slopped back to the stables in her rubber boots. Or was she just good-humored? It was hard to tell. If she told on us, at least they'd go in the wrong direction.

I looked at the gray and white house for the last time. But I couldn't see if anyone was looking out of the windows. The sun climbed over the opposite ridge, and its rays stung my eyes. In the morning this was the sunny side of the valley.

The rays weren't warming a thing yet. It was awful to sleep and walk around in the same clothes.

Teddy looked a little pale and stiff, but he got more lively after we'd passed the henhouse behind the barn. The cock was crowing, and that was a new noise. He seemed to think I'd made it. When he heard a second "cock-a-doodle-doo," he nudged me in the ribs and almost died laughing.

"Doooo," he mimicked, and folded up. I had to steady him. The chuckles and clucks that followed would have been envied by the most cackle-struck hen. Naturally, I'd have preferred to steal away silently, so I tried to speed him up a little. But I also fooled around and pretended to be a hen, because it was important to keep Teddy in good spirits.

Had it rained during the night? No, it must be dew. Our feet got soaked—grass grew in the middle of the farm road and spattered drops of water on our shoes.

I tried to forget my stiff toes, and when we reached the gravel road again, we didn't stamp and jump just to get warm.

Yippee. Now they wouldn't be able to see us from the farm. Only the cock called us. "Diddle-diddle-oo."

I danced and bounded, and Teddy hobbled after me, full of fun.

"Morning is a golden time, morning is a golden time. Hi! Hurrah for teddy bear, who is so good, so rare!" My words fitted Teddy's favorite song, and sure enough, he said, "Pippurra," with many ha-ha's afterwards.

When Teddy hears his song, he always cries, "Pippurra."

I'd never understood what people mean when they say a morning is golden, but the dewy fields did look as if the sun had splashed them with gold and silver. Even the weathered wooden fence had a golden look about it.

But my morning mouth didn't feel very golden. It was full of unbrushed teeth and bits of hay. If we found a brook, I'd dig out our toothbrushes. I'd nearly lost them in the hay last night when I'd taken out . . . the raincoats!

We'd left them in the barn. I turned the rucksack inside out, but no coats. We'd left them in the hay

111

with our names and addresses on them. What great calling cards!

A dog barked, and below us the farm suddenly came to life. A tractor was driven out of a shed, and far down the hill the cows were being sent out to graze.

I didn't dare return and get the coats. It was too late.

"We'll forget about them, Teddy. It's no use wondering who'll find them and what will happen."

"Pippurra?" suggested Teddy, with his head cocked. That meant more song.

"Sure, sure. Hip! Hurrah! We're almost at the forest, and, look, the table's been set. We'll eat fresh berries for breakfast."

I snatched some blueberries from the bushes that grew on a level with my head along the side of the road—that's how steep it was. Oh, well. They tasted like cold, sour water. They were soggy too. But the crowberries looked delicious, and there were mounds of them. Big and bright red.

"Today's the day the teddy bears have their picnic." I didn't remember all the verses, but I made some of them up. What fun. Singing and tra-la-laing make you happy, especially if you're making someone else laugh.

If I fooled him just the tiniest bit with a deep bear voice, Teddy gasped with delight. Yes, we managed quite a few curves through the forest on that picnic.

Sometimes I thought the teddy bear padding after me was a good, kind one. He's clumsy and lumpy and big, just like a bear. But he hasn't got those cunning little bear eyes.

Even in the bright sunlight I wouldn't have felt very brave if a real bear had poked its snout out between a couple of pine trunks.

Grrrr, came from down the hill, and around the rock on the last curve I saw a snout—a car snout.

I hotfooted it up the slope with Teddy in tow. A car was almost as dangerous as a bear.

I flung the rucksack down on the heather and said, "Pick berries, pick berries, yum yum, nice berries. Here, Teddy."

We bent over a tuft of crowberries, so all anyone could see from the car when it passed was a big and a small behind in bluejeans.

I squinted between my legs and the berries. What a nifty sports car model. Two youngish men and another snout—a white and brown dog's head against the window—sat in it. *Grrr!* Then they were gone.

To think I hadn't heard the engine. Served me right for bawling songs at the top of my lungs. Besides, the hill and hairpin curves swallowed the noise. Already I could only just hear the roar of the engine.

The men hadn't looked as if they were searching for a couple of boys. "No cause for panic, Teddy."

He wandered from one bush to another, picking berries with his thumbs and forefingers. He squashed the blueberries, which squirted, and the crowberries were too slippery for him to hold.

"Wait a minute, and I'll pick some for you." He got a handful, but most of them fell on the ground.

It was a quarter to nine, a good time for breakfast.

The heather was still wet, so we trudged to a clearing in the forest. There were no lumberjacks in sight, but logs were crisscrossed in every direction. We sat on a trunk that had been almost entirely stripped, and it gave us a wonderful view over the valley. We'd certainly come a long way up.

The clearing was about level with the highest farms on the other side of the valley. Over there it wasn't so steep, so the farms were higher than on our side.

The barns had white walls and red or black roofs, and the houses were stained brown or painted white. The fields, too, were different colors. Some had been plowed already and some were just about to be plowed. We saw tiny tractors and horses. Other fields were pale. They looked almost white from where we sat.

I thought the whole thing looked like a giant crossword puzzle, only someone had pulled the dark and light squares of earth a little out of shape.

While I buttered slices of bread and made crowberry sandwiches, Teddy watched a herd that had been driven to the forest. They were grazing in a hollow below us. The cows looked like the toy animals in our chest at home. Teddy stretched out his hand, but I don't know if he meant to catch a cow.

114

Their lowing echoed from rock to rock, making the herd sound much closer than it actually was. Teddy, of course, tried to imitate them too. "Yes, you're clever." I gave him a nod, but kept my eyes and ears open. No more surprises, thank you!

We'd be better off following the path from here on, I decided. The road made too many wide sweeps. And we might run into more cars.

"Mick too," Teddy said after the second double-decker sandwich.

"I don't have millllk, But you can have some blueberries." At least they were juicy.

He threw away the berries I gave him. "Mil-llk," he said carefully and looked beggingly at me. I was thirsty also, so I packed the rucksack and promised to find us something to drink.

We stumbled over some twigs and broken branches before we found the path.

Teddy didn't seem very happy. He wanted a drink of milk, and he didn't want to move. But when he answered a moo that came from the cows in the hollow, I clapped my hands and praised him so much that he began to giggle a little.

So he mooed some more and clapped his hands, and we managed to climb a couple of steep slopes.

The path suddenly rose almost vertically. It was so steep that Teddy only had to lean forward a little to rest on the ground.

We'd have to make hairpin curves into the woods and back. Maybe the road wasn't such a bad idea, after all, especially as there were so many roots and stones in the heather that I had to support Teddy to keep him from falling all the time.

It got hot, much too hot for sweaters and parkas. We couldn't just walk in the shadow of the trees, and hitting a sunny slope was like walking into a furnace. I peeled a couple of layers off us and pushed the clothes into the rucksack. Teddy flopped down on the grass. "Pooh."

I loked hopelessly at the gray crag that hung over us. We had to go even higher than the crag and much farther. I could have done it in an hour and a half, or two hours if I took it easy, but with Teddy I couldn't cover the distance very quickly.

What was the strange smell—ants?

Yes, Teddy was sitting practically on an anthill that was just behind him, and he was swarming with giant ants. They crawled around him and up him. He must have parked himself in the middle of their main street.

He didn't notice the ants until I dragged him to his feet, but as soon as he saw black, shiny, crawling things on his hands and arms, he set up a roar.

"Take 'im away, take 'im away." He waved and jumped so much that I could hardly get near him. Flick, flick. But some of the ants had sneaked inside his clothes. There were screams and shouts as he felt them.

"Easy now, take it easy, wait a minute." But it isn't exactly easy to unbutton the shirt and pants of a live jumping jack. He carried on as if a thousand ants were crawling over him.

I found one or two, but even after I'd shaken them off and buttoned his clothes, Teddy squirmed and wriggled. He looked as if he were trying to brush away more ants.

"They *are* nasty, aren't they. Come on, let's run away from them. Far away!" Poor thing, he swallowed it cold—trudged beside me as fast as he could, and that was a good deal faster than before.

"See, you *can* do it." But I knew his dawdling wasn't just the result of moodiness. Mrs. Breden had said something about muscles that weren't fully developed, but I must have been daydreaming at the time.

Oh, yes. Mrs. Breden. What did she think of us? Did she think we were safe and sound in Uncle's cottage now? I had the feeling she didn't.

"Heh heh." Teddy's tongue hung out, and he panted terribly. "Is nuff." With that he stopped short. Father usually says, "No, that is enough," when Teddy has carried on too long.

We'd worked our way around to the top of the steepest bit, so he really did deserve a rest. I took a branch and swept the ground, slapped it and patted it with my hands. "All right. You sit here. No ants."

It didn't matter what I said; he didn't dare sit down, even though the little clearing was covered with long, soft grass. It didn't smell of ants, either, but of lovely warm summer forest.

"Mick." His lips were dry, and I'd heard some

kind of trickling or murmuring behind the rock we'd
just rounded.

"Will you wait here a minute, Teddy?" No
answer. He'd cocked his head, and he looked as if
he were listening to something quite different.

"Maybe I can find us some water. You stand there
or sit down. I'll be back in a minute."

"No." He protected himself with his hands and
whimpered.

"But, Teddy, there aren't any ants here. And I'll
be back in a minute. Aren't you listening?"

But I was the one who should have listened to
him.

His whimpers followed me as I darted among the
spruce trees and across a mossy ridge. Well, it
couldn't be helped. It would only take me a few
minutes. And down in that hollow there must be a
river bed.

I couldn't hear the sound of water. . . . No, I
couldn't see any water, either. Over the next ridge,
then. I stepped on some reeds that went "suck, suck"
with every step. I must be getting near.

I jumped from one tuft to another. Some of the
tufts nearly caved in when I jumped. Now I could
see the water as well as hear it.

It was only a thin little worm of a brook, wriggling its way through a broad bed, with a couple of
little pools here and there.

I lay down on a flat stone bordered by brown,
slimy weeds and stuck my face into one of the pools.

My knees got wet and I got a lot of water up my nose, but it was good to quench my thirst. What could I use for taking water back to Teddy? I'd forgotten to bring the wooden ladle that hung behind Father's rucksack.

But the plastic bag for the bread was still in my pocket. I filled it and twisted its neck a couple of times before I began to jump back.

Halfway up the slope I started, and the water splashed. A deep lowing came from—from the clearing where Teddy was sitting. Now he would get frightened again. "Teddy," I called. "Don't be afraid. I'm coming."

Too late. I charged through the bushes toward the little pasture and saw the top half of Teddy backed against a tree. Three enormous cows moved slowly toward him from different directions.

He opened his mouth, but he couldn't make a sound or move.

"Hi! Git! Shoo!" I pushed, prodded, flapped my arms, squirted water.

The cows drew back a little in a leisurely way and stopped.

"They're going, Teddy. Here I am, here's Mikkel. Look at me."

But he pulled a face, screwing it up as if he were in terrible pain—and he probably was too. He stared fixedly in one direction, and—help—there was a pair of horns coming out of the bushes. And another pair. The whole herd from the valley came toward us.

I am *not* afraid of cows. Not much, anyway. But as the whole herd started milling around me in a few yards of grassy meadow, I decided that looking after Teddy was pretty rough work.

The nearest cows just shook their heads when I tried to chase them or push them away. They behaved as if I were a fly that had settled on their noses. They didn't get very worked up about the prods I gave them; they lowered their horns and looked as if they meant to butt me, and the only thing I could do was jump back.

And those large eyes and those moos. You can never tell what kind of mood cows are in. One dark, dappled cow with a white skull head did look fierce. It waddled straight at me and blew air at me through its nose. It didn't pay any attention to what I told it. We had to get behind the trees.

Yes, *we*. Teddy had locked himself. He was stiff and hard as a board and wouldn't budge. A cow nibbled at his shoe. I could hear Teddy huffing and wheezing like an engine.

"Okay, take *that* and *that*." I kicked out at the white flank. The cow took it as an invitation to follow me again, and I leaped behind another tree. Now the cows were a little further away from Teddy. As long as they kept away from him, I could sprint from tree to tree until doomsday.

We were caught, squeezed by a wall of heaving backs—a sight to make anyone turn pale. What could I do with these mounds of meat? Their tails swished in a crazy rhythm all the time and their jaws did too. Tug, champ, champ, champ, and the tufts of grass disappeared. Oh, what a mob!

"Git," I yelled. "Can't you eat grass somewhere else?"

One of the light cows made a leap toward me, and I had to dash for cover again. "Crazy cow. Fatty guts." It was a wonder the cows didn't get the giggles watching me jump up and down and scold them.

Then I heard someone call from the path below, and suddenly the cows behaved as if they needed exercise. Their bodies started moving, their heads changed direction, their bellies swung—the herd scattered.

I turned to see who'd rescued us and felt pretty small—our savior was a little girl who looked a lot younger than me.

She ran the cows with a stick and hit two half grown calves that wanted to bound into the forest.

"You're not afraid of cows, are you?" she asked, out of breath, and stroked the strands of hair over her eyes.

"Afraid?" I hoped she understood that it was hilarious to think I was afraid.

"I'll chase them so you won't be frightened any more," she said, soothing me. That's how much I'd convinced her.

"I can chase them myself. . . ." Luckily she didn't hear me.

"Shoo, off you go," she called, and flicked her

stick at the rump of a lazy old cow that was ambling after the others. It bellowed, insulted, and broke into a trot, making its whole body flap and shake.

The girl informed me rapidly that the leader with the bell had done something or other on the way back from the mountain pastures, so now she had to take the cows to the pasture when she wasn't going to school.

Small and eager, she carried on about how they were soon going to give the bell to another cow, and then she wouldn't have to accompany them. Her hair hung around her face in strips—frizzy, spiky ones over her ears and normal ones over her forehead.

She suddenly realized that the cows had disappeared. "I'll have to run," she said, and away she ran with her dotted dress fluttering under her red sweater, a bright red spot among the brown tree trunks; and then she disappeared into the forest too.

I turned to Teddy.

He was vomiting. He often vomits when he's been scared.

"Now, now, everything's all right."

There wasn't much water in the plastic bag, since I'd squirted most of it at the cows. I washed his face, and he drank what was left in the bag.

It would be no use trying to climb another hill just yet. "We'll rest awhile. Come on."

I strolled away from the cow manure and stretched out in the sun where the forest sloped a little. No anthills? No. A tiny ant scurried across the pine needles, but I hoped Teddy wouldn't notice.

He followed me and dumped himself down beside me, sat close to me, almost on top of me, and didn't look around at all. But he had his feelers out. He started at the slightest sound in the wood, even the twittering of a bird. And if I tried to move, he complained and clung to me.

He must have thought that I'd chased all the cows away! I was glad he didn't realize what a sissy his brother was.

"I'll chase them—if any more come," I boasted, and tried to sing. But it didn't have the same effect. He neither liked nor disliked it. Didn't say anything, didn't do anything, just sat.

This would never do. At any moment people might come searching for us. The little cow girl could tell them where we were.

I thought I knew where we would hit the brook. It took a left turn and would probably cross our track a little further up.

"Isn't it hot, Teddy? Shall we go bathing? Bathing, Teddy?"

After repeating the questions several times, I managed to get him moving. "Bathe bathe," he said over and over again as we climbed the path—or rather, the cow track.

We waded, splashed, and washed ourselves. Teddy cheered up a lot, so I didn't mind him getting wet. He looked quite calm and good-humored when I tied his shoelaces later.

123

"Now we're ready. We'll follow the brook up this cleft, and we'll arrive in about an hour."

Did I really believe that? I didn't stop to think about it.

"Keep going, Teddy."

9

They Come After Us

One hour? Wishful thinking. Four, five, six hours.
The whole day.

Walk, rest. Climb, rest, rest. Walk again, drink
water, rest.

As long as we followed the brook, I could make
up games to amuse Teddy. We sailed ships of bark,
built a dam, and tossed sticks and pebbles into the
water. But then the brook stopped wanting our
company. It heard a friend on the left-hand side of
the gully and hurried to meet it. Nonsense, of course
—I know perfectly well that brooks run downhill,
but sometimes the water did look as if it were
climbing.

There was nothing to do but fill the plastic bag
with water and wave good-bye to the brook. "Take
the mosquitoes with you," I called.

The mossy ground and thick pine woods ended,

and we entered a belt where there were more leafy trees than spruce. The air was alive with buzzing. The mosquitoes probably hadn't noticed that the leaves had turned red, although the cold nights should have scared them out of pretending it was summer.

The view got better as we worked our way up the mountain. The valley and hills reappeared between the crooked grayish-white tree trunks and the curtain of leaves. At first we saw Malberg in little glimpses, but then we saw the whole town. The river that had run so furiously under the bridge looked frozen from where we were. It stretched out like a green road of ice. If it had actually been frozen over it would have made a wonderful skating rink.

Oh! I'd thought we'd seen the last of the farms when we stopped in the clearing strewn with timber. But high under the top ridge of the mountain sat a lot of little gray farms.

Above them rose peak after peak and ridge after ridge. The higher they rose, the more bare they were.

The mountains nearest us were covered with stubble, apart from a few bare patches where the stubble had been covered by landslides.

Tooot, came from below. "Look, Teddy, the train." I pointed to a toy train, which was drawing a line along the side of the valley. The smoke from the engine looked as if it had come out of an icing gun, like the one Mother uses to decorate cakes. It curled over the engine, then loosened and got broader. Further along it sent up only a couple of little blobs, the last drops to be squeezed out.

I couldn't count all the times Teddy said, "Nuff," and flopped down on the heather. He had to be coaxed after every rest. I started him by singing and by giving him food—berries, water; I started him by playing; I threatened him by talking about the cows. It was cruel, but it helped.

To think that taking a rest would ever make me feel exhausted! My throat and head felt as dry as desert river beds, if such things exist. Next time, I thought, I'll give in too, and lie down and let things take care of themselves.

But then it got brighter ahead of us!

The birches became even shorter and more twisted, and changed to greenish-white willow thickets and juniper. Now the path was not so steep. Well, not quite as steep. A last short scramble skyward, and then . . .

You almost feel as if you're in a church when you're on top of a mountain and you see the mountain world around you. It's enormous, tranquil, and strong. Little scatterbrained people should stay away from it.

But instead of asking God to forgive our presence, I congratulated Teddy and myself. "We're up. Look at all this."

He merely followed my hand with his eyes. I can save myself the trouble of pointing unless there's a hooting train or moving object to catch his attention.

How I wished he could see the plain, marshes,

lakes, moors, and the row of snow-capped peaks in the distance, piercing the sky. And all the colors! I never could have mixed any like them in my paint box.

Teddy didn't even enjoy our first glimpse of Uncle's cottage at Vingomli.

Hweee, the wind swept over us now that there were no ridges or rocks to deflect its force. We already had our sweaters on, but I got out our parkas as well.

There are four huts at Vingomli. Uncle's cottage is the newest, so it was easy to see it.

"That's where we're going to live, Teddy. There'll be an open fireplace and a nice bed and warm food, yum, yum."

He looked around as I zippered his parka. He probably thought the food was near us.

"No, first we've got to walk there. It isn't far. Come on." I started off with new strength.

Teddy didn't seem to have new strength, or old strength either. But he'd heard what I'd said about food and kept insisting that we should " 'ave lunch" and "go 'ome."

All I could say was "Sure" and "Yes."

We were visible wherever we walked on the bare scrub, so I trotted over to the road.

"Come here," I called, waving. "It's not so hard to walk here."

No. He bent his head and scowled at me.

Think of something better. Dive into the rucksack

again. I broke the heel of our last three-quarters of a loaf and held it in the air.

"Food. Food for Teddy."

He slouched toward me, grumbling sulkily, showing no interest. Oops! He slid on the edge of the road and needed help. Once we were in the middle, I handed him the heel as a prize—as if it were a new and exotic dish.

He glanced at it sourly and threw it away. I dived into the heather and fished it out. We might need every crumb.

Teddy marched ahead of me in a huff. Fine! Just keep going.

I was eager to know if anybody was living at Vingomli. If people were, we wouldn't go there. But no matter how much I stared I couldn't see any smoke winding above the roofs. It looked as if the huts up there were as empty as the two we were just passing, which were asleep with drawn shutters. Each hut had a little wooden fence around it. Good night.

How quiet it was in the mountains. Traffic and city noises—did they really exist? The wind whistled, the moor whispered, and the dwarf birches shook their tiny leaves. But a blanket of silence covered all the little sounds. It was a bit eerie.

A thick bank of clouds rose over the sun setting in the west. Soon it would get dark. We had to hurry. We had to find shelter before the angry clouds behind the mountain ridge reached us and poured water on our heads. They were rain clouds, I could see.

"Shush." I stopped and held my hand in the air, although Teddy hadn't said a word. There was a new sound in the air, and it buzzed through both the blanket of silence and the wind. We weren't all that far from traffic and city noises, then, because I was listening to the sound of an airplane.

It was still flying behind the bank of clouds, but it was coming nearer. It had never occurred to me that they might search for us by plane.

We had to reach cover. But there was nowhere to hide. Not a decent tree or rock on the whole moor.

Suddenly a dragonfly flew through the clouds. It wasn't a jet but a little single-engine plane that dipped over the ridge.

I dived into a thicket of willows, but Teddy stood in the middle of the road and looked almost as invisible as the mountain.

"Play hide and seek!" I roared. "Hide yourself."

He obviously felt that we'd played enough hide and seek coming up the hill, but when I kept badgering him, he thrust his arms out and sighed, "Ohhh, well, well," just like me. Guess if I recognized myself!

I don't know whether he was trying to copy me or looking for a place to hide, but he slid down the loose embankment again and ended up in the ditch.

"Stay there," I shouted as loudly as I could over the drone of the plane above us. Was it my imagination or did one of the wings tip slightly as if the people inside wanted to look at us? How much could they see as they whizzed above the earth?

"All clear!" But Teddy wasn't interested in games. He lay on his stomach and played with the dirt he'd pulled down with him. Earlier in the day he'd enjoyed kneeling and poking his head behind a bunch of heather or a bush. As well hidden as an ostrich, he'd peered out with a broad smile when I called him.

But there was no happy "titt-ttee" now. Just grunts and grumbling.

"You *must* get up, Teddy. We've got to hurry." The plane had made me nervous again. We were so unprotected on the moor. We might be observed from several directions without our knowing it.

It took about half an eternity to get him moving.

The weather was freezing. The parkas helped to cut the wind of course, but some gusts pried through the openings. And my fingers felt like blocks of ice. I flapped my arms and thumped Teddy on the back, but he didn't like that at all.

A little tear appeared in the bank of clouds. The sun had set, but its reflection bathed Vingomli in red. All around us were masses of black clouds, but above Uncle's cottage and the surrounding moor, the reflection flared like . . . danger. Another stop signal!

The last remains of the day sky made the little lakes glitter. I think there's a fairy tale or something called *The Troll Mirror*. Now the landscape looked as if the troll had dropped his mirror and it had splintered in a thousand tiny pieces.

We *weren't* alone in the mountains. On the banks of a lake I saw three dark figures with fishing rods. They moved toward the road a little ahead of us.

The best thing was to dawdle, then. We couldn't very well throw ourselves on the ground, because they'd probably already seen us. If only they didn't cross our path!

But if they didn't come, that meant they lived at Vingomli. . . . That would be even worse. No—the road to Modalen made a fork just beyond the lake, I suddenly remembered, although we couldn't see it from where we were.

"Go to Modalen." I tried to hypnotize the fishermen.

I couldn't tell where they went, for the clouds thickened, and the light faded. And then it was impossible to make out anything.

I stood and held Teddy's arm. All he said was "No." I tried to listen for voices from the direction on the lakes. Silence. I felt so cold that we finally had to move.

"Nooo!"

"Yes, just a little more, Teddy. Clever boy."

He dragged his feet after him and shuffled, and the dust blew into his face. Was someone turning the bend? No. Had I heard a whistle? Yes, the snipe over the water. Either the fishermen were ahead of us on the road or they'd gone toward Modalen. Otherwise, we'd have met them by now. The last slope up to the cottages couldn't have taken most people more than ten or fifteen minutes. But Vingomli was still dark half an hour and three quarters of an hour later. So they must have gone to Modalen.

We reached the fork. And then the mountain rose ahead of us again. What difference did it make that it was the last hill? We'd never climb it!

Teddy hooted his long "noooo" whenever I touched him. He hadn't uttered another word for more than a couple of hours. He couldn't walk more than four steps at one time.

"We'll freeze to death tonight if you don't move." I pushed and pulled, but it didn't make me warmer either. The wind was rising and the clouds were coming closer.

You could sense the roofs and chimneys against the night, but the sky was black, black. What was that? A twinkle of light? Or was I seeing a star? I stopped and held my breath. A gleam immediately disappeared.

It must have been someone holding a flashlight. I saw two beams of light—a car!

The beams cut straight at the sky for a while; then they flattened out. The car was climbing the road toward us. Two yellow eyes glared.

Had the pilot seen us and informed the people in the village? Anyone would have had time to find us with all the time we'd taken—snails.

No, I mustn't get panicky. We were on a road; it was natural that cars would use it. Quite natural,

Mikkel. People who weren't traveling to Modalen might drive past Vingomli and on to Dalseter, even though it was easier to reach it by another road, the road we hadn't taken, the road we'd told the girl at the farm we were taking. . . . Oh, shut up.

There was no time to think. Here we were, game on the run, and a car was coming after us. I searched wildly for a hiding place. The heather was too short to conceal us, and the bushes by the side of the road grew too low.

"Come here, Teddy." By pulling and dragging, commanding and scolding, I managed to get him off the road. I kept my eyes on the car lights all the time.

Two sharp beams of light swept over the moor in wide arcs and then stared straight ahead.

I saw a large rock quite near us. I mightn't have noticed it, except that it cut off the light for a moment. That rock became our goal. I dug my teeth into my lower lip and used all the strength I had, plus all the strength I didn't have, to drag poor stumbling, moaning Teddy behind me.

Between the gusts of wind I could hear the hum of the engine. The car was going downwind. Then it changed gears—and didn't turn toward Modalen. It started climbing toward us again.

In that case it was a matter of minutes. I'll make it, I'll make it, make it, make it. Over the last stretch I more or less carried Teddy. Don't know how. Knew I had to, and so I managed.

Exhausted, my heart throbbing somewhere in my

throat, breathless, I flung myself down behind the stone. Teddy collapsed without a sound.

It got horribly light, but the rock shadowed us. I couldn't even find the breath to tell Teddy to lie still. He did anyway.

I caught a glimpse of the car. It looked like an Anglia. Don't know anyone who owns one. Didn't see one at Malberg either.

Drive on, don't stop at Vingomli. Drive!

But, no. The Anglia slowed down, as if the driver didn't know where to stop. It stopped at Uncle's cottage.

Well, I might have known. They had to find us.

It was raining. I hadn't noticed. The rain poured down in bucketfuls. The lights were still shining, but I could only see the outlines of the car and the two people who stepped out of it and ran over to the hut. Two oblong figures through the rain.

The scene reminded me of a television program just before "Sorry, due to a technical fault . . ."

If the people were going to enter the cottage, they'd have to break in. The key was in the rucksack.

One of the oblong shapes reappeared. I could hear voices—first a man and then a woman's. But I couldn't make out whether the man's voice was Father's or whether the woman spoke with a Danish accent. I'd have run up to them if I'd been sure they were Father and Mother. They wouldn't want Teddy to be locked up.

The oblong shapes moved here and there. I decided to crawl closer and find out what was going on.

Teddy lay on his side and breathed in even snorts. He must have fallen asleep. He wasn't getting very wet, because the rock sheltered him, so I took a chance and stole away.

I wormed my way carefully up the slope, but a worm would certainly have found it easier than I did. Either my behind stuck up in the air or my shoulders did. The juniper needles stung my face, the twigs scratched and cut me, but I kept trying to hear the voices.

I tightened all my muscles and tried desperately to hear through the splashing rain and the gusts of wind. Finally I felt as if I had an iron rod through my head. Maybe I'd only heard the woman's voice in my imagination. All I could hear now was a faint mumbling behind the car.

Ugh, I was soaking wet. Leaves and little twigs stuck to my hands.

Suddenly the shower slackened and I could hear everything more clearly. I peered over a clump of heather. Yes, it was easier to see now too.

The smaller shape didn't belong to Mother. Mother's thinner, and she never wears slacks. The other shape resembled a tent more than anything else. No, it couldn't be Father. His coat is shorter, and his shoulders are broader.

"They must be at a farm, then." As soon as I caught the words, I knew who'd spoken. Mrs. Breden!

"Yes. They couldn't have walked this far," the man answered, but I didn't know his voice.

Hweee, another blast of wind and rain whipped my neck, harder than before.

The oblong figures got back into the car and slammed the door. I lay flat as a flounder, with my nose in the moss, while the Anglia backed and turned between the cottages. Then it rolled slowly down the road.

The brakes shrieked—was the car about to stop? No. Maybe Teddy would wake up and make a noise. No, he didn't.

"Cloudy, with some patches of fog and rain," bleated a hoarse radio, as the wheels scrunched past me. Gravel and grit struck the fenders—*scrump, scrump, click.*

But Mrs. Breden didn't stick her head out and cry, "What on earth is that lump over there? Mikkel!"

The car drove on, weather forecast and all. Down to the village drove Mrs. Breden, and she would tell the world that there was no one up at Vingomli.

I should have jumped for joy because they hadn't found us. We would be left in peace now.

But I felt lonely and lost, as I squatted and followed the red rear lights with my eyes—two glowing drops of blood that mingled with the rain in a dim blur for a moment before they were washed completely away.

10

Alone

Teddy, you've got to wake up. We're almost at the cottage.

But you're all wet. You're just lying in a pool of water, a bathtub. The water's running down both sides of the rock and over you. You're soaked. Oh, what would Mother say!

Please, please, get up. You've got to. Up.

Come on, get up. Help me a little.

Lift your feet. That's right!

Fine. One more step and another—no, watch out!

Did you fall? Well, I'm not crying, so don't you. It's worse for me; I've got to get you on your feet again.

Maybe I am crying, just a little.

I give in. . . . I won't make it. . . .

Just a little further, Teddy, two more . . .

* * *

It must have been a dream. It couldn't have been the cottage door I was banging my head on. I must have imagined it.

Because I was lying dead on the ground. I was sure I was. Dead.

But . . . maybe I could get myself on my knees, just out of spite.

Oh, they felt so sore!

If I had the strength, I could get the rucksack off my back too. The key was inside it. The big cottage key.

But my fingers were dead.

When you can't untie a knot, the best thing to do is to take your knife and cut through the rucksack.

What was roaring next to me? Oh, yes, Teddy.

There were two lamps on the kitchen counter. Matches.

Wood, kindling, and newspaper were stacked in the fireplace, ready to light.

Come to think of it, I was alive. Alive.

Although it was pretty hard work dragging Teddy into the living room.

A thin tongue of flame ate its way through the paper. *Frrrot!* The paper flared up, and then the whole fire blazed.

Hot gusts swept over us. But the smoke?

I should have remembered the damper.

The smoke didn't choke us. It stopped after a few minutes.

Clothes get glued to your body when they're wet,

and it's practically impossible to undress people who're lying down.

I threw our clothes in the corner near the fireplace.

Swoosh, flop, they fell.

The blankets were hanging in the bedroom alcove.

I felt warmer after I'd rolled them around myself in front of the fireplace.

Or did I actually feel cold?

Turn out the light, someone. . . .

11

A Knock on the Door

I could have slept for another six months, at least.

If only the movers hadn't dumped the furniture on top of me. The leg of the couch cut into my stomach, and the piano crushed my chest.

Help! Air!

The "furniture" was Teddy. I was kneaded like bread dough on the floor as he tried to get up, on top of me!

"Get your knee off me." As if I didn't hurt enough already.

Once I'd had to have my arm broken again because the bones hadn't knit properly. This time I had to break my whole body, it was so stiff.

Teddy tottered among the furniture stark naked. He bumped into the wooden armchair, grasped at the handle of the mug on the mantel. I managed to pry the mug out of his hands while he stood swaying.

"Come and sit on the couch." He pulled the blanket over himself again, and I pushed the table in front of the couch—to keep both Teddy and the blanket in place.

The day had dawned, but the windowpanes were so steamed up that I had to rub them to look out.

And then I saw that it wouldn't help to rub them, because the fog was so thick around the cottage that you couldn't see a thing. Well, you could make out a little. The wooden fence around the next-door cottage and the shed were a bit darker than the gray fog.

My watch . . . had stopped. Trust me to forget to wind it.

There was a smell of—what was it—train soot? No paraffin smoke! The lamp had burned out, and the wick was dry. We must have slept a long time, because the paraffin lamp had been full when we arrived.

That kind of smoke could be dangerous, although we seemed to survive everything.

They couldn't have walked this far, the man had said. Ha ha. I don't think Leif Arne would have managed or Karsten or the others. But Mikkel the fox had managed.

I beat my chest and jumped around to get warm and bawled out a sort of Tarzan-like yell.

The mirror in the alcove made me shut up. Nobody would have mistaken me for Tarzan's twin brother.

142

I found some mountain-climbing clothes of Uncle's behind the curtain. Clothes belonging to my aunt too. And in the bureau I found Uncle's underwear and socks.

I quickly shut a drawer full of women's underwear.

Our clothes were still scattered in wet lumps on the hearth. I would light a fire soon and hang them up to dry.

"First we'll get dressed, Teddy. We can look around later."

He looked pretty awful dressed in Auntie's mauve cardigan and Uncle's pants tied around his waist with a clothesline. But I looked worse. I had to hoist my pair of pants to my armpits with the help of suspenders, and even then I had to roll up the cuffs. But the plaid shirt and leather vest helped a bit.

I waltzed around the room in an enormous pair of shoes. Teddy would have stumbled in them.

"Lift your foot, and we'll put some socks on you.

"What's this mess? Oh, dear." He had a big, raw wound on his heel.

"Poor Teddy. Did you walk with this all yesterday without saying a word?"

Without saying a word! I laughed to myself scornfully. He'd tried to say a great deal, but I hadn't listened to him.

"I think Uncle has a first-aid box in the corner cupboard, or maybe it's Auntie's. Look, here it is."

I talked without stopping, because I couldn't stand the silence.

"Iodine and bandage. There, you'll be fine. Now it doesn't hurt any more, does it?"

Teddy didn't look as if he noticed any difference. "Let's go outside for a few minutes."

There was a faint smell of gas in the kitchen. "We're going to cook a meal soon. This gas stove is great. It's a good thing I helped Father cook up here, because I know how to work it," I said.

Uncle's rubber boots were on the porch, and Teddy didn't protest when I helped him put them on.

I couldn't help shuddering. The scab around the wound must have been very painful.

He didn't even twitch his nose. "You *are* tough, Teddy!"

It wasn't very far to the shed, the shed Father and I had built. I knew every plank and could almost feel a groove in my shoulder from carrying them. They'd laid in a supply of firewood since I'd been here. It was stacked up to the ceiling. "At least we won't get cold."

The fog was great. Nobody would be able to tell if smoke was coming out of our chimney or not. Nobody would see what we were doing.

"Marvelous, Your Majesty."

His Majesty wouldn't stay in the shed. He got terrified when he saw the big dark hole of the privy and realized that it was very deep. He'd never sit down on it!

I took an armful of wood back to the house and gave Teddy a log. He just dropped it.

144

He dragged his feet slowly and followed me through the stiff rushes, coughing and grumbling. He obviously didn't like the sour, foggy air.

"Bend down, Teddy." No, he *would* have to ram the door with his head.

He said nothing, but I heard the wallop. "Did you hurt yourself?"

He seemed to be all right. "Clever boy. Come in so I can shut the door."

But he didn't move. The Dutch door was unfamiliar, but he didn't fiddle with it, didn't swing the upper part and the lower part in different directions as he would have done ordinarily. He just stood there.

Of course, I couldn't expect him to be very energetic today. We were both worn out. And hungry!

"Come in, and we'll find some good things to eat in the cellar." I tried to tempt him. No, that wasn't a good idea. He'd probably fall down the ladder.

"Wait there, Teddy, and I'll get some food. I'll be with you in a second."

And with that I locked the porch door. But although Teddy hadn't wanted to come in when I tried to wheedle him, he certainly didn't want to be left outside now. He rattled the door knob and called, "Noooo."

I hurriedly opened the trap door and climbed down the ladder. A flashlight hung from a string on the ceiling; a genius must have left it there.

The cellar was just a damp, stone cave. Father

was planning to build shelves and shutters for the windows. The preserves were stacked on crates that had already started to moulder. The cans were rusty and the labels were falling off, but I was sure this wouldn't affect the contents.

The beam of the flashlight glided from corned beef to fish cakes to hamburgers, peas, meat. Yum! Condensed milk, jams. There was plenty to choose from.

"Would you like hamburgers, Teddy?" I called. I only got thuds and sobs for an answer.

"We've got some money. We'll pay," I told the cans of sardines and hamburgers that I took down. We could live for a long time out of cans—eight or ten days maybe.

And what then? asked a cheeky voice. I felt as if I had a radio transmitter inside me. But I didn't want to think. We'd eat and relax. I slammed the trap door, and the whole cottage shook.

"We're going to have a wonderful time, Teddy." He was leaning on the door, and I had to push him away to force it open.

"Wasn't I quick?" I only got a sad, hangdog look. He wouldn't take his boots off, so they came in with him—flop, flop.

"Now, now, Teddy, I'll get you something to eat. We're safe." Just for a while, said the transmitter inside me, but I turned it off.

The can opener wasn't very good, but I managed to pry loose a half circle and shake the hamburgers into a pan. Then I lit the gas.

"Don't get in my way all the time. There isn't all that much room in this kitchen." He looked so shocked at the jab I gave him. "Look, we'll light a fire in the fireplace too, so it'll be nice and warm in here."

I flapped my arms to make the log catch on fire —there wasn't enough of a draft. I tried the bellows. Teddy clung to me and made it hard for me to get near the fire.

"Why can't you sit down somewhere?" For once he was obedient; he collapsed in a heap. "No, get up again!" He'd almost put his back in the flames. "You mustn't sit in the fire. Dangerous."

He never pays any attention to things he should be frightened of.

I couldn't have been quick enough, because I smelled something burning. Not wood or paper. "What have you scorched? Uncle's pants?"

No, the hamburgers!

Some cook I was. Fortunately, not all the hamburgers were burned.

I found a package of crackers in one of the cupboards. They weren't exactly crunchy or crispy, but I didn't care. We were too hungry.

I put the pan on the hearth. I'd already gobbled up one helping and was laying into another when I realized that Teddy was just moving around the bits I'd cut up for him.

"Aren't you hungry? Yum, yum, food." Yesterday he'd moaned for food endlessly. But now, with a delicious, only slightly burned dinner on his lap, he didn't want any.

"Maybe you're thirsty?" That must be it. Where would I find water? In the well outside.

"You sit still and wait. . . . No, you'd better come with me."

We returned to the kitchen. The pails were on a shelf by the door. "Bend your head." He got through the door all right. I ran ahead of him with the pails, because the well was in the hollow near the neighbor's house. It had just been dug and held so little water that no one could have drowned in it.

I managed to half fill the pails. You didn't need coffee to color this water!

But Teddy wasn't thirsty either, although I tried to skim off the mud. A couple of sips were all he'd drink.

He wouldn't open his mouth to eat, even though I held the spoon and said "Yum, yum" for all I was worth. He didn't say, "Nuff." He just pushed the plate away.

Oh, well. I managed to eat the hamburgers myself, even the burned crusts. And the crackers. Boy, they tasted good.

"Now we can sit by the fire and relax." The fire blazed merrily, crackled, and rustled, and I had to put the fire screen around it. I hadn't bothered the night before. It was a good thing no sparks had fallen on us. The cottage might have caught on fire, too.

But . . . behind the chest against which the fire screen had been propped . . .

"Yabbadabbado, Teddy. Look! A transistor radio." With a battery! Great.

I switched it on and waited, opened it up and made sure the wires were in place. Waited.

Dead. The battery was dead.

How irritating. I wouldn't have minded, if we could have only listened to the police messages.

Now I wouldn't find out if Mrs. Breden had come up here last night because we were wanted by the police. But why else would a stranger leave her home and children late at night? Surely not to say hello and see whether we were comfortable.

Usually it's a real job to keep Teddy away from a radio. He loves twiddling the knobs until he gets music and "pippurra." But the transistor radio didn't interest him at all.

"Isn't this a stupid radio! Sit down, Teddy."

He should have felt comfortable in the armchair after I'd adjusted the high back and wrapped a blanket around him. But something was definitely missing.

He didn't lay his head on my arm while I tucked him in or nudge me playfully and laugh himself sick afterwards. He didn't hum, talk to himself, didn't try to copy what I said and did, didn't smile. Everything that makes it nice to have Teddy around was missing.

"Does your foot hurt a lot?"

A log rolled down and made fireworks. The whole roof might have fallen in as far as Teddy was concerned.

Sure, we were all right. Much better off than yesterday. We were in clover, dry and warm. We had a house and beds.

But sitting and staring at the fire got a little . . . monotonous. Too peaceful. And my lousy transmitter kept squawking inside me.

If they hadn't broadcast our descriptions on the radio or newspapers, we could drag ourselves over to Modalen after a couple of days. For I had to confess to myself that we weren't too safe in Uncle's cottage.

We didn't know anyone in Modalen. I could find work on a farm, if someone wanted an unskilled farm hand—a farm hand who had to take care of his brother. And if they hadn't heard about us of course. Oh, switch off!

"The more you rest now, the sooner we'll be able to go away." I didn't need to ask Teddy to rest. He was asleep.

That was unusual too. Must be the mountain air. Father says it makes people sleepy.

But how convenient! People are no trouble when they're asleep.

I paced the room, walked over to the window with the checked curtains.

Well, well, the world was beginning to get a bit bigger. Now I could make out the fence stakes and a piece of the road, the door and shutters of the neighbor's cottage. But the fog was still thick. It was impossible to believe that yesterday we'd been surrounded by mountains and wide spaces.

If the men in the airplane had spotted us, they'd know we were up here somewhere. If, if, if. Turn it off.

I gave the transistor radio another kick. Everything was going wrong. The radio I needed didn't work, and the one inside me was cackling away full blast.

There were books and some magazines on the middle shelf of the corner cupboard. I marched back to my chair with something called *No Mercy!* that boasted a lurid jacket—a grinning mask and a hand with a dagger.

But it was like trying to do homework when the lines sort of roll along on belts, to return over and over again. I never know what they mean. A lot of thoughts pop up between them.

Mack the detective bundled up his papers and turned off the light in the office . . .

Where were Mother and Father? What did they think? Were they frightened? Surely they understood that I couldn't let Teddy be locked up.

Mack the detective bundled up his papers and turned off the light in the office again, *but as he was about to . . .*

Mrs. Breden had certainly been kind and meant well, but she ought to look after her own children. . . . *turned off the light in the office, but as he was about to leave—*there was a knock on the door! No, I hadn't read it. I'd heard someone knock. There was another knock. On our door!

12

Fever

Who was knocking? I couldn't see. The door was at the back of the cottage.

What should I do? Jump out the window? Throw a rug over Teddy and hide under the couch?

They'd know we were here. The chimney was smoking. The door wasn't locked.

Be a man, Mikkel.

It's not easy to walk with firm, sure steps in shoes that are six sizes too big.

Lift the latch on the porch door. Bang!

"There *is* someone at home," said a voice.

I opened only the top half of the door, straightened my shoulders, and stood on tiptoe.

Two ladies switched on their smiles at the same moment. Elderly, not too good-looking.

"Excuse me, can you tell us if that path over there goes to Dalseter?"

"No, not over there, Klara. That's the path we just climbed."

They pointed and waved. They didn't have a clue about Teddy and me or compass directions.

"You'll get there more quickly on the main road," I said in as deep a voice as I could muster. "It's over on the left."

"You see, Klara? The main road, I said."

"I guess you didn't listen to me, Martha! We'd better not go out at all, I said, until the fog has cleared up. It's hard to find your way in the fog, you know."

I waited patiently for them to sort things out and find their way. I nodded sideways at what they said and managed to peer at their wristwatches. Ten to twelve? No, upside down, Half past four.

Martha insisted that the fog had started to clear before they left "and the radio had predicted good weather."

I stiffened, but they didn't say another word about the radio. They didn't say a word about two runaway boys roaming the mountains. Maybe our descriptions hadn't been broadcast, after all.

"Well, we'd better get started, Martha, if we want to reach the hotel in time for dinner at six."

You'll never make dinner, I thought, but bowed and said, "You're welcome," when they backed away, thanking me. "Have a nice walk," I even added, out of sheer kindness.

I felt like a dignified property owner after I'd closed the top half of the Dutch door.

The Dutch door was a great invention. If they'd seen me with Uncle's drawers rolled up and his shoes, I wouldn't have looked quite so dignified.

Merry as a flea, I hopped over to Teddy. "Just a couple of twin aunts who were lost. Don't know if they really were twins, of course, but they sure looked like twins."

I'd wakened him up. "I forgot you were asleep. Are you all right?"

He was *not* all right.

He drew himself in with a shudder, and his eyes looked so strange—they were large, staring eyes, almost like a doll's.

I felt his cheeks. Their color was fresh enough, but they were boiling hot. His forehead too.

"You've got a fever, Teddy." He must have had a fever. He wasn't just tired and worn out after our long walk.

"Do you want to lie down? Go to bed properly?"

He huddled up in the chair and bent his head as if he were trying to escape from something. He whispered something I couldn't hear.

I ran and pulled some bedding down from the rafters in the alcove. We didn't have sheets, but I put a thin blanket on top of the mattress. As I placed the pillow and comforter in the bottom bunk, a scream came from the hearth.

Loud and long. It sounded like a cow lowing in pain.

I ran back and put my arms around his shoulders,

while he pressed himself into the corner of the chair and pushed at me with his hands.

"Take 'im away," he called several times.

"Yes, I'll take them away. There now!" I hit the empty air and groaned a little at the same time. "Now they're gone, Teddy. All gone."

At least it was easier than making real cows go away. I didn't know, of course, if he was seeing cows, but it seemed to help. He breathed out, and I got him out of the chair.

"We'll put you to bed, Teddy. It's nice to sleep in bed."

"Yes, thank you," he said, so meekly and correctly that I nearly jumped.

His fingers felt like hot dogs. His knees folded up and I had to work to drag him. Pull him a little, rest against the table, over the threshold, rest, drag him to the bed. Whew!

I sank down on the comforter, and he laid his head on the mattress. He seemed to think he was in bed.

It took a lot of wriggling and heaving before his whole heavy, slack body was in place and most of his clothes were off.

Then I tucked a blanket around him. "Sleep well. Smile at me, can't you? Smile at Ellik?" He's always said "Ellik" and I've never wanted to correct him.

But he didn't smile. He shivered, and his teeth chattered.

He'd feel better if he drank something hot. Soup!

Mother used to make us soup with fruit syrup in it when we were ill.

But how did she make the soup? It was strange, but when I went into the kitchen to look for something soupy, Teddy called, "Motha" after me. Just as if he could sense that I was thinking about her.

"I'll be there in a minute," I answered. Poor thing, he didn't know how far away Mother and Father were.

The light was getting so dim that I had to light a lamp. The little flame looked as if it were trying to help keep all my sad thoughts at a distance. What if Teddy got really sick now? What would I do?

Aunt Helga's cupboard was practically bare: some tea, coffee, sugar, and oats in jam jars, and tomato soup in cans.

Tomato soup—no, that wasn't right. I needed oats. A ladleful of muddy water and a shower of oats in a saucepan. Teddy moaned as I lit the gas.

I took the lamp and shone it on him. What was the matter with him? He didn't cough, and he didn't seem to have a cold. What was wrong with people when they got ill?

Measles? That's what he probably had. He must have been infected by the Breden family.

I put the lamp on a chair. "Let's have a look at you, Teddy."

I unbuttoned his jacket and looked at his chest and stomach, but there were no red spots on them. No, they wouldn't appear till later, till the fever died down, Mrs. Breden had told me.

I could see his heart beating, a little bump that rose and flattened out, quickly, quickly. I laid my head against the bump and heard thud-thud-thud. It was no use counting the beats, because I didn't know how fast his heart should go.

Teddy trembled and shivered, making the bunk shake. He shuddered as I buttoned him up. My fingers must have felt like icicles against his burning skin.

"Now you'll get some . . . soup!"

It had boiled over, of course, and put out the flame so that the gas whistled into the alcove. That was all we needed—to be poisoned. Ugh, what a stink.

I thought I'd better air the room by opening the door and windows, because Father says a cottage can explode if you strike a match and the room is filled with gas.

Meanwhile I had to pour more water on the cereal. That's what it had turned into—cereal, not soup. Teddy kept whimpering in the alcove. He sounded as if something hurt him. But what? What?

"Is your head sore, Teddy? Does your throat or stomach or back hurt you?" How awful that he couldn't tell me.

Suddenly I remembered what Mrs. Breden had said: "Teddy might get very ill if he got the measles." She probably hadn't dared to tell me that he could die from them.

Now I knew the danger signals *had* meant something—this. But, actually, I'd known it all along,

I'd known what I'd done was crazy. Danger signals, bah. Rowan leaves and sunsets and all other red things weren't extraordinary. I was getting carried away by superstitions. Transmitters inside me, pooh! The voices were just things I fooled myself with when my bad conscience got too troublesome. That was all.

My hand shook so much that far too much sugar fell into the soup. I added cold water to cool it off.

Teddy seemed a bit better. He said, "Ellik!" as I handed him the soup. It made me so happy. Maybe everything would turn out all right.

I put an extra pillow behind his head and then another, because it's hard to drink when you're lying down. And oh, how thirsty he was! His appetite was very different from his indifference at lunch. He squirted and spilled the soup but emptied the whole cup. He wouldn't give me the mug when I tried to take it.

"I'll bring you some more. Then you'll get well. Isn't that right, Teddy? You feel better now?"

The cup, he wanted the cup. "Yes, yes, I'll hurry."

There was barely a cupful in the saucepan, but fortunately the jam jar was still almost full of oats. "I'll make more soup later on."

But when I returned, balancing the cup and the lamp, he didn't have the strength to lift his head. He just lay back with his mouth open, with dull, half-closed eyes.

"Soup, here's your soup." I needed three hands: two for lifting and supporting his head, one for pouring the soup into him. No, it just oozed out of the corners of his mouth. Forget it.

I grabbed a towel and wiped his neck, and suddenly he fell asleep—went out as if someone had pulled the plug.

I tiptoed out of the room and fixed some more soup. He might drink a lot during the night.

The night. I couldn't bear to think about sitting up with my sick Teddy all night. It was already so dark that I had to light a lamp in each room to see where I was going.

You've done a great job, Mikkel. Dragged Teddy with you into the hills, miles away from help.

Some responsibility I'd shouldered. Not a performance to be proud of.

After I'd made the soup, I walked from window to window. But it was like staring into the saucepan —just thick soup outside, made with brownish-black water. There wasn't a sign of life.

Wasn't that typical. Now I would have welcomed with open arms all the people I'd tried to avoid: Mrs. Breden, the villagers, the fishermen, yes, even those aunts from Dalseter.

If Teddy had gotten ill a little earlier in the day, the women might have carried the news to their hotel. There was a telephone there, and the doctor might have been here by now.

"Hhhhh." I rested my forehead against the windowpane, and my head thudded and thumped, not as quickly as Teddy's heart, but it seemed to drag me down.

He whimpered and thrashed about in the bunk.

He wasn't quite awake, but he kicked and struggled to throw off the comforter. His face was bright red and even hotter, but he wasn't sweating. Yes, the blanket was wet . . . oh, yes. Everything was soaking wet.

It wasn't surprising. He often does it at home too, even when he's well. But there we have an oilcloth under the sheet. If only I'd thought of putting something on top of the mattress, like the plastic raincoat hanging on the wall, for instance.

It took me a long time to pull away the wet blanket and get his clothes off. He moaned and carried on whenever I went near him.

"Does this hurt you? I've got to change the blankets."

He hit out wildly as I struggled to change the bed.

I couldn't do anything about the mattress, so I got a bundle of newspapers from the wood box and eased one under him every time he moved. He resisted if I tried to push or roll him.

I wrapped a dry comforter and blanket from the top bunk around him. "But what am I going to put on you? You can't lie there with nothing on."

Back to the fire, which was about to go out. Yes, his shirt was dry and so was his underwear.

I threw two logs on the fire and puffed a little at the sparks with the bellows. The flames burst out immediately. We wouldn't be sitting around the hearth much tonight, but I'd better make sure that the house didn't get too cold.

A wheezing like the sound the bellows made came from the alcove, only Teddy's breathing was shorter and quicker. Teddy sounded shorter of breath than he had climbing the steepest bits of the mountain the day before.

I still couldn't see a rash on his body, but he shrunk away from me and his teeth chattered when I tried to put his shirt on. "Frrrrrkkugh."

I wished I had something warm to put in his bed. Maybe I should heat some water and pour it into a bottle. That's what my grandmother does when her feet get cold.

But I had to run back to him. The scream that cut through the cottage didn't sound like any of the earlier ones.

Teddy arched in the bed like a bridge and turned white.

And his face, his eyes!

13

Help!

Help! was all I thought. Help, help, help!

I didn't dare touch him, go near him. I was almost as stiff as he was with fright.

"Don't scream, please. *Please*."

But he didn't shut up. The screams continued. Was he being cut into little bits?

I put my fingers in my ears and staggered over to the corner cupboard.

The box with the medicines. I must find something that would help.

"Be quiet!" Only dry sobs came from my throat as my fingers fumbled among the jars and tubes.

Couldn't see what—couldn't see what was written on them. Had to take them to the lamp.

The jar wouldn't stay still. It jumped in my hand so that the label was il—illegible.

Pull yourself together, Mikkel. Hold on to the edge of the table.

One to two tablets to ease pain, it said. Headache, toothache, rheumatism, neuralgia. I couldn't believe anyone had ever suffered what Teddy had.

If I doubled the dose, gave him four tablets, and then ran, ran as fast as I could for help . . .

Suddenly everything was quiet.

My ears sang, and I had to swallow.

Dizzy and faint, I staggered toward the alcove. I held the jar so tightly that I almost broke it.

Yes, he was still breathing.

He lay pale and quiet with drops of sweat on his forehead, cold sweat.

He only just moved his eyelids when I dried him carefully with the corner of a towel.

I couldn't see getting him to swallow the pills. I'd have to wait until he got a little better. *If* he got better.

How quickly could I run down the main road to Dalseter? Or down to Modalen? Not fast enough.

Hours and hours would pass before I could find a doctor and bring him to the cottage. I couldn't leave Teddy alone for a couple of hours, not for a quarter of an hour.

What about sending some kind of signals? An SOS with the flashlight? I could build a fire outside, a big warning blaze.

Who would see it? Nobody.

Even if there were people up in the hills, the night fog was like a wall around us. No fire could penetrate that darkness, not even if the cottage itself burst into flames!

The hut—flames—gas—

It started again! He stiffened, and his terrible screams rang through the rooms.

I couldn't bear listening to them. I wanted to race through the kitchen to the porch, past the shed, onto the road, and call with all my strength into the wall of fog.

Help! Help! Help!

I won't turn on the gas now, Teddy.

If you die tonight, I'll be a murderer anyway.

But, later, then I'll do it.

I'll fill the cottage with gas, strike a match, and ... that'll be the end.

Forgive me, Teddy, for everything. I'll stay with you.

14

You'd Better Drive Fast!

How light it was suddenly.

The light was blinding.

There was probably going to be an explosion. I'd hear the bang soon.

Yes, there it was. But it wasn't a big bang. And I wasn't blown through the air. Because it was the noise of car doors banging, and the light came from the headlights of the car.

Car. I didn't know whether I was awake. Better to stay beside the bed, with my head on the pillow and my cheek against Teddy's.

"Arrh-mmm, arrh-mmm." His breath kept ending in gasps.

"Mikkel!" It was Father, outside.

"Teddy! Mikkel!" inside.

I opened my mouth and called, "Yes," but I couldn't make a sound.

"They *are* here. The lamps are burning, and they've made themselves some food, and . . ." Now Uncle Bjarne was talking.

The alcove got dark again. Father's bulk almost filled the door. Father is broad. His head and arms were framed by light.

"Yes, they're . . . both here." He sounded as if he had a cold—hoarse.

One, two steps, and he was across the floor, and I was in his arms. His hands squeezed my shoulders so hard that I nearly had to yell.

"Are you all right? Is Teddy asleep?"

Father bent over the bunk.

"Sick? Has something happened to him?"

"M-me-measles." The word finally spilled out.

"What?" Father barely managed to look surprised. His eyes were small and tired, and there were heavy bags under them.

He turned again to Teddy and called him. He put his hand on Teddy's forehead and laid his ear against Teddy's chest.

Then he straightened quickly, almost hitting his head on the edge of the upper bunk. He swept over the wet bed linen on the floor and out. The floorboards jumped as he ran.

The car lights had just been turned off, but Father called, "Wait a minute, Bjarne. I think we'll have to . . ." The rest of his words ended in mumbling beyond the cottage.

Father had arrived.

He'd taken on the responsibility.

167

I felt empty inside. Empty and dead.

The darkness of the night glared through the windows, and the lamp reflected itself in them.

But only my body sat next to the bed now. My real self sat further away.

There sits Mikkel, I thought. Mikkel doesn't move.

Father returns with Uncle Bjarne. Father points, first at Teddy in the bed, then at Mikkel.

"Doesn't look too good," he says.

Uncle Bjarne walks over to the bed, pats Mikkel on the head, feels Teddy's hands.

Then Teddy stiffens again, and Mikkel knows what's coming. He clears out—Mikkel's clever.

Before the screams have started, Mikkel is sitting on the hood of Uncle's van—not the Volvo.

A few minutes later Uncle comes out, dragging a mattress and blankets. "I'll have to get rid of the junk in the back so Teddy can lie there. Were you very scared?"

Mikkel doesn't answer.

"I think it's called a fever cramp. One of our children used to get it when he was young. Torkel, I think."

Rattle, thump. Into the cottage with a box and a roll of tarred paper.

Torkel's in the navy now. He has a gorgeous uniform.

Uncle comes out of the cottage backwards. Father and he are carrying a long bundle of blankets between them. The bundle squeaks and moans, as if there were a puppy inside.

"He's very ill. You get in first, Harald. I'll keep him steady."

The van shakes. I hear bumping and thudding. The puppy howls. Then everything is quiet.

"I'll go put out the fire and scatter the ashes. You'd better stay here."

"Hmmm. Bring the wet blankets. And the things hanging by the fire."

"Don't worry about the blankets. Oh, well, we may as well take them."

Uncle goes in.

Mikkel waits in the car.

Father walks around to the front of the van, opens the door, and gets in beside Mikkel. The seat rocks.

Father pulls out his pipe. The tobacco pouch. Starts packing the pipe. Clears his throat. Puts the pipe in his mouth, but takes it out again.

Mikkel waits.

"Did you want to . . . run away? From home?"

He says it so clumsily. Father seems to have as much difficulty finding words as dumb Mikkel. . . .

Then I saw that it was no use running away from responsibility and myself.

"I had to take Teddy away from home."

"What?"

"Yes, I left you a note. I didn't know what else to do."

"What note?"

"The one I left in the kitchen on the stove."

"Haven't heard of any note. It might have blown away."

"But didn't you understand when you heard what happened on the field?"

"Did something happen on the field? What happened?"

I only saw Father's profile against the faint light that came from the cottage window. His jaws worked as I told him about the game with the Biters and about Stig and his teeth.

"He just lost a couple of teeth?" Father relaxed and put his pipe and pouch on the dashboard.

"Y-yes, and he split his upper lip. Do you think that's *just*?"

"No, goodness, that was plenty, but it could have been much worse."

"But didn't the police talk to you?" I asked twice.

"Eh? Yes, of course. We had to tell them you'd disappeared."

"Yes, but—" Teddy seemed restless and groaned. "He can't lie there alone. Shall I—?"

"No, you stay here. Look,"—Father wrapped his coat around me—"you probably did the best you could, Mikkel."

He didn't say another word, just climbed down and walked over to Teddy. Father, who can get so angry!

Then I really unwound. In the dark, in the front seat, in Father's coat, I sat and cried. Warm streams poured down my cheeks. They tasted salty, and I didn't have a handkerchief.

But when I saw that all the lights had been turned off in the cottage and Uncle was standing at the door with the flashlight, turning the key, I rubbed my eyes on my sleeve and stopped sniffling.

They talked behind the van, while they threw the clothes in and Father made himself comfortable beside Teddy.

Uncle seemed to know everything I'd said.

"Didn't know any better. After all, he's not very old," said Father.

I was *not* going to cry any more. At least Uncle wasn't going to catch me crying.

It was true that I didn't understand an awful lot. But not because I wasn't very old.

"Well, well, so you weren't just taking a jaunt through the hills," said Uncle, as he sat behind the steering wheel.

"No!" Had they really thought that? Thought that I'd almost killed Teddy and myself just to have a vacation in the cottage?

Then they were the ones who didn't understand very much!

Uncle started the car and backed onto the road. How well I knew every tuft of grass we bumped over. You try and drag your brother over them, Uncle, I thought.

Father poked his head through the little hatch behind us.

"Bjarne! He lives near the bridge. I just remembered."

"The local doctor?"

"Yes, but don't you think we should drive straight on? As fast as we can?"

"Drive straight home?"

"Yes, and get Dr. Brun to look at Teddy. He knows him."

"No, no, it's too dangerous. We've got to take him to the nearest doctor." I couldn't help joining in.

"What do you know about it, Mikkel?"

"I know it's worse for Teddy to get measles than for other people. People who have brain afflictions get much sicker."

"What? Brain—hfff." Father snorted, embarrassed. "Teddy's quieted down, Bjarne."

"Teddy might die."

"Now, Mikkel."

"Well, I don't know," said Uncle. "Five hours is a long time. Shouldn't we see the doctor just to be on the safe side? Seems sensible."

"I guess so." The latch was closed.

"It's a good thing we have the van. Quite an ambulance," said Uncle.

Ambulances must have better springs. We bumped and rattled down the twisting road, and I could hear Teddy screaming. He wasn't being very quiet, after all.

"I should have sat in the back."

"Try to rest a little, Mikkel. Everything's fine. When did you reach the cottage?"

172

"Last night, or maybe it was the day before . . ."

Uncle pumped me about our journey and our climb up the mountain, mostly to stop me from listening to Teddy's screams, I think.

My head smarted every time he moaned. And every bump seemed to cut into my forehead.

But I had to ask what had happened at home. Why hadn't the police looked for us?

Uncle told me everything he knew.

Mother thought that we'd taken the loaves over to Grandmother when she saw that two of them were missing, and that we were having lunch with her. That's what we do usually.

Around bedtime, Mother went to the telephone booth and phoned. She discovered that we hadn't been at Grandma's.

"Your mother should have called me right then. I could have taken charge, as I have a telephone at home. But I didn't know anything about it until the next day."

"What about Father?"

"Of course, you wouldn't know. Someone backed into the Volvo while Harald was visiting his last customer in Sundby. He had to take the car to a garage and stay in a boarding house. Your mother didn't know what had happened to him either, so she was quite beside herself in the evening."

Poor Mother.

She'd rushed around searching for us for several hours before she told the Nilsens, some people we know. The whole family had helped her search, but they hadn't phoned the police until early the next morning.

"They should have called them at once," Uncle Bjarne said.

The police had organized search parties to comb the woods near the house. Yes, they'd dragged the lake too. "Naturally, everyone said you couldn't have gone far."

"But didn't you see that the key, the cottage key, was missing from its hook?"

"The key? I didn't even know that Harald had it. And there was no one at your home, remember? Your mother sat next to our telephone. And Harald took a train after he'd called me from the office to tell Jenny he was all right and came over to our house. Well, that's enough about all that. . . ." Shortly after one o'clock the first bus passengers had heard the news and had informed the police that Teddy and I had gone to town the day before.

Then the police had intensified the search and broadcast our descriptions over the radio at half past six.

"And about an hour later the police chief at Malberg called us to say that a Mrs. . . . a Mrs. . . ."

"Breden!"

"That's right. The lady who'd been on the train with you. She said you looked desperate, so she was expecting the police message."

Desperate, pooh! I'm not a gangster.

"The police chief said he'd go and find you, because Mrs. Breden had told him that you'd said you were going to Vingomli. Then we began to see the light too. So Harald stopped the search, and we drove to Malberg to find you."

But when they'd arrived in the middle of the night, the police chief told them we weren't in the cottage. Father and Uncle and some of the people on the neighboring farms had scoured the hills for the rest of the night.

Early in the morning they heard that our raincoats and a teddy bear (I'd forgotten all about Winnie-the-Pooh!) had been found in a barn. They talked to the girl we'd met, and naturally she'd told them that we were heading for Dalseter. So they'd enlisted the rescue workers and searched all the countryside around Dalseter.

"Harald and I helped. We looked in the forest and on the plain, but in this fog . . ."

Uncle's voice started to sound a little foggy. My eyes were closing, and I didn't have the strength to open them.

"What about the airplane? Didn't it spot us?" I asked, hardly moving my lips.

"Eh? Plane? Yes, we did see a plane, but it had nothing to do with us. But then in the afternoon, no, evening, some hotel called up and said that two of its guests had seen a boy in one of the cottages at Vingomli. . . . blah . . . blah . . ."

Thank you, twin aunts. So they'd found their way back.

"Blah blah blab blab . . . threw themselves into the van and . . ."

175

I couldn't bear to go on listening. Couldn't bear to see, talk, hear. I should have asked about Stig and why his parents hadn't said anything to the police, why no one had said anything . . .

Too tired. Pains all over, not just in my head.

Teddy was feeling lousy too.

This old garbage van was rattling us into a thousand pieces.

The hatch opened. Father: "We'll have to see the local doctor, after all."

Uncle: "Thought so. Blah blah . . ."

Oh, Uncle, don't talk so much.

". . . but I've told you hundreds of times that it's too big a burden for Jenny. Teddy should have been put in a home long ago . . ."

"No!" I managed to say "No" twice. Uncle didn't care about Teddy.

Oh, stop shaking, car! Stop turning! I'm feeling sick.

Finally we stopped. Don't slam the door.

". . . no need to carry him into the house. I'll crawl in and take a look at him . . ."

". . . measles? Hardly. . . . both lungs . . . to the Central Hospital. I'll phone them and give him an injection first. Good-bye, and you'd better drive fast."

15

Home Again

You'd better—you'd better—you'd better drive fast.
Drive fast!

No, don't!

Not around the bends. Everything's turning over,
ohhhh. . . .

". . . didn't know you got carsick, Mikkel. Here,
take this handkerchief."

Can't take anything. Stop! Slowly! Brakes!

The world is racing, racing into outer space with
a roar. Stop!

Someone lifted me like a baby.

Father's voice: ". . . both of them. Pneumonia."

Mother's voice: ". . . Mikkel. Don't you know
Mother?"

Sure. Of course. She's the only one who says
"Motha" like that.

* * *

But the knife cut my chest so badly when I breathed.

Couldn't breathe in—ouch! Sore all over.

And they boiled me. In a pan. With herbs. Hot. Bubble, bubble . . .

Thirsty!

Teddy's gone. I know he isn't here any more. The house is empty.

I killed him.

"Mother!"

"Did you say something, Mikkel?"

Eyes too heavy to open. Weigh a pound each. The lids press down.

Grandmother is sitting by the bed. Not Mother.

"She's at the hospital with Teddy."

"No. He's dead. I've killed him."

Grandmother just shakes her head.

Dr. Brun sticks a syringe into me. Time after time.

"Mikkel, you've got to drink a little of this. Your mother made it for you before she left."

Gruel with fruit syrup. I know all about it. . . .

Tastes good—great. I drank the oats at the bottom too.

"That's right, that's better." Grandmother smiled. Kind blue eyes behind her glasses. Kind eyes that looked like . . .

"Where's Teddy?"

"He's in the hospital. All we can do is hope he'll get better. Hope and pray . . ."

*　　*　　*

Then Mother came. She hugged and patted me, said I was clever and had to hurry up and get better.

"Teddy?"

"We're still hoping."

Her freckles were yellow and her face a light gray —cement. Eyes red-rimmed.

Father's cement was darker. More like sand and water. His cheeks hung down, making him look like an English bloodhound.

"Everything will be all right. We can only hope."

I hoped and hoped, but didn't know exactly what I hoped. Hoped Teddy would get better, of course. But afterwards?

What would happen? Everybody must know everything by now. What would they do to him?

I couldn't trust Uncle Bjarne.

It was better to lie back in bed and not think at all . . . look out the window at the falling leaves, fluttering as they fell.

Fell.

16

What's Going On?

Teddy came home the day I got up for the first time.

I staggered down the stairs, holding the banisters with both hands, and saw him in his bed, pale and thin.

But he smiled when I entered his room.

"There," he said. As if he'd expected to see me every time his door was opened.

"Thank you," he said too, and handed me a banana he was about to eat.

I didn't really want it, but I took it because he was so happy to give me something.

I sat in the wicker chair in Teddy's room while Mother fixed lunch. We were both so weak that we just sat. The wicker chair went creak, creak, creak.

I handed him a magazine. He nodded and smiled again but didn't look at it. Didn't even look at the great boat on the cover.

I didn't have the strength to hold the magazine, so it fell under the bed and there it lay.

It was good to have him home. But . . .

Later on his bed would be empty. I wouldn't be able to visit my brother when I got up in the morning.

Don't think about it, I told myself. Think about Christmas.

But Teddy wouldn't be with us, wouldn't stand in front of the tree and look as if he were in paradise, wouldn't look ecstatic if he touched a tinkling bell.

I couldn't switch off my transmitter.

Something *was* going on, something had been decided that I wasn't supposed to know. I sensed it all the time.

They'd probably decided that Teddy should be "situated," as Uncle puts it. Locked up, I call it.

Uncle kept dropping over at the house.

"We're going to eat, Mikkel."

Father was already sitting at the table. He hadn't come in to say "Hello" first, as he usually does.

He chewed his bread, and his jaws worked sideways. He too was thinking. He always chews that way when he thinks, whether he has something in his mouth or not.

"Hello, Father."

"Oh, hello, Mikkel. Nice to see you on your feet again. A bit shaky, eh?"

"Yes."

181

And Father chewed and stared into his glass of water.

Mother served the stew. From then on she looked into the air.

So I had to ask. I didn't want to be left out of it any longer.

"Have you talked to Stig's parents, Father?"

"Um." Father took a swallow of water and nodded. "With *him,* that is."

"With his father?"

Another nod.

"Was he angry?"

"His father? No. Nice man. He understood."

"Then what's happened? What are they going to do? Haven't they reported it?"

"What? No. We'll fix it up between us, his father and I. They'll get some money from the National Health Service."

"Stig will need a false tooth, but the dentist thinks he can save the other tooth." Mother obviously thought I needed a little more information.

Father had gone over to see Stig's parents, she explained, and they'd told him that they'd thought of mentioning it to him. They'd had to take Stig to the out patient department, where his lip had been stitched, and to the dentist. His mother had been very upset.

But the next morning they'd heard that Teddy and I had disappeared, and they hadn't wanted to trouble Mother and Father. They'd asked other people not to mention the accident either.

"Yes, but then . . . then the police don't know a thing about it, do they? So it's as if nothing had happened? I mean, Teddy can stay at home, just like always."

Even before I'd finished talking, I knew from their faces that nothing would ever be the same again.

"We've been discussing that recently," said Father.

"Eat your food, Mikkel," said Mother.

"But you can't do that. If we don't have to . . . You really don't want to . . . Don't you want him at home any more?"

"Yes, yes!" Mother picked at her napkin and looked even redder around the eyes. "It isn't easy for us to decide."

"There's a new home . . ." Father chewed.

"A new home they've just opened."

"But this is home for Teddy. I promise I'll look after him. It'll never happen again. You can't really do this." The words tumbled out and got muddled up.

Father lifted his hand. "You'll have to let adults take care of things from now on. You've arranged enough already, I think."

So I got it straight.

Then Father dived into his plate and refused to say another word.

I looked imploringly at Mother, but she shook her head.

"We haven't decided yet, Mikkel. We don't even

know if there's room. Uncle Bjarne is going to find out for us, and . . ."

Uncle Bjarne, naturally. Just as I'd thought!

He's always harangued us about putting Teddy in a home. I'd have to talk to Uncle. Mother and Father no longer listened to me, since I'd brought them so much trouble.

I felt sweaty and dirty. And my back, arms, everything felt like jelly.

Both Mother and Father had to help me upstairs to bed.

17

Leif Arne

The next day I staggered around the kitchen garden for a while, dragged my feet through the slimy leaves, and looked at all the work I'd have to do. The work I should have done . . .

I figured out how long it had been. Nine days. I'd missed a week of school after the fall vacation.

It didn't matter much. I'd catch up with the others in no time. Actually, I always have too much time at school; that's why it's so dull.

Maybe Father intended me to start the next day. But I didn't like that idea. I had to stay home and see that no one came to take Teddy away.

They probably wouldn't come yet. They couldn't lock up someone who was ill. They weren't all that brutal, were they?

Ouch! I'd kicked the hoe, which was lying under a pile of weeds.

I picked it up and loosened the earth around a turnip slightly.

"Mikkel!" someone called from the gate, and Leif Arne scurried over to me through the red currant bushes.

"Hi! Are you outside?"

"No, I'm sitting in my room." It wasn't a very friendly answer, but the other boys hadn't done much to help Teddy or me when we were in a tight corner. I didn't want them to forget it.

Leif Arne stopped and picked some leaves off a bush.

"Picking turnips?"

"I'm not digging for gold, anyway."

"Do you want me to do it for you?" He edged over to me cautiously. "You've been ill, haven't you? Pneumonia?"

"Yes." I handed him the hoe as if I were doing him a favor.

"Is Teddy better too?"

"No. He's in bed."

"Isn't he well yet?"

"Ohhh." I groaned at his questions. He was about to burst with curiosity—that much was obvious.

Go ahead and burst. I don't care.

My head spun when I stooped, so I didn't pull up any more turnips. I sat down on the wall of the basement stairs instead.

Leif Arne followed me, dragging the hoe behind him.

"Why are you like that?"

186

"Like what?"

"Sort of grouchy. Won't talk."

He bent forward and leaned his chin on the handle of the hoe. His whole carrot top was perched on the handle. If I kicked away the hoe, he'd fall on his chin, ha ha.

"If you guys had shown some more guts and helped me in the field, nothing would have happened."

I couldn't be bothered to go on. It was hard work talking to people. It was wearing.

"We helped you, all right. We fought the Biters, Karsten and me. Bredo, too."

"I didn't see you."

"Nope, you weren't there. You'd gone. So you couldn't see a thing."

"Did they make a fuss after we'd left too?"

"Sure. We clobbered Stig's pal, when he said he'd call the police. And then the others pitched into us. A couple of guys were bleeding after *that* fight."

"Were they?"

"They sure were. You bet."

It was clear that I'd been unfair. But even so I couldn't bring myself to say anything nice.

Somehow I was even angrier with Leif Arne because there was nothing to be angry about.

"What have Stig and the rest of the Biters done to you?"

"Done to us?" I asked.

"Yes, didn't they report it and isn't Teddy being

sent away? That's what everyone's saying. They say he has to be locked up."

"You're lying. Everyone's lying. It isn't true. They won't take him!"

I yelled so hard that Leif Arne backed away and let both the hoe and his chin fall.

"Okay, okay. But that's what Stig's mother said when she drove off to the out patient clinic with Stig after he got hit. He looked awful. No wonder she was mad."

"They changed their minds afterwards. You can go tell everyone that it's a big, black lie."

With that, I marched into the house, leaving Leif Arne—went straight upstairs and threw myself on the bed.

Was that the real story? Had Stig's parents just been polite to Father? Were Father and Mother lying to me just to make me keep my trap shut?

A "home," they said.

Home, my foot.

Prison!

18

Uncle Bjarne

A car stopped in front of the house. Father?

I got out of bed. No, Uncle, with Aunt Helga in tow. What did that mean?

I peeped at them from behind the curtains, as they stood talking to Mother. She'd opened the kitchen window, which is just below mine.

"Yes, Harald must be on his way home. I hope you'll stay for dinner."

"Oh, no, thank you. We've got to fix supper for the children. But I've brought you a dozen eggs." Auntie Helga held up a round basket. "You can scramble them for the boys. Can I go in and say 'Hello' to Teddy?"

"Please do. I'll open the door."

They nodded and walked toward the house. Aunt Helga is several sizes larger than Mother, so she looks better beside big, strong men like Father and Uncle.

Scrambled eggs—the very words made me feel full.

I opened the door a crack to hear what they were saying in the hall. Shush! The hinges needed oiling.

"Meanwhile I'll sit on the veranda and roll myself a cigarette. I want to talk to Harald, because Mrs. Breden phoned today. . . ."

Oh, yeah! So Uncle Bjarne was ganging up with Mrs. Breden, was he!

Pretty crafty.

I heard Mother and Auntie going into Teddy's room.

Then I'd better attack Uncle immediately, pronto, while I felt furious, and brave!

Clump, clump. I didn't tiptoe down the stairs. Why should I?

Past the living room, out to the veranda.

Tendrils of ivy waved around Uncle, and a cloud of smoke curled sideways from the bench on which he sat.

"Hi there, Mikkel, old boy. Great that you got better so quickly."

"Not all that quickly."

"Oh, you've been coming along nicely. Soon you'll be as strong as you were when you carried planks to the cottage."

"What did Mrs. Breden want?"

Uncle's cigarette was halfway to his mouth, but he let his hand fall. Ashes showered over his pant legs.

190

There! He obviously didn't know what to answer.

"Mrs. Breden—yes, that's right, you know the woman, don't you?"

"What does she want?"

"Well, it's about Teddy. Mrs. Breden has been wonderful. She can get him into a home—but you'd better talk to your mother and father about it. They're the ones who'll decide, after all."

"Did you ask Mrs. Breden to arrange to have Teddy sent away?"

"I beg your . . . pardon?"

He'd heard me perfectly well. He was just stalling. So I repeated the question, loud and clear.

"No . . . yes, I suggested it. But actually, she asked me first. She wondered whether Jenny and Harald would be interested in some kind of arrangement."

"You needn't have agreed. You *know* we want to keep Teddy at home."

"You shouldn't get so worked up about it, Mikkel. Sit down." Uncle pulled me down on the bench beside him, because I'd been standing, waving my hands in his face.

"If it can be arranged, it's the best thing that could happen. For everyone. The whole thing had to be straightened out. Teddy can't hang around home all his life. I've said that many times."

"Of course he can. It's been fine up to now. Well, apart from Stig, that is; but his parents haven't insisted we do anything. And I'll look after him—"

"Surely you understand, Mikkel, that it's far too

big a burden for your mother. For Jenny! To do all the housework and work in the garden and do the sewing she has, without a minute's peace from Teddy!"

"I look after him as soon as I come home from school."

"Well, well, but you'll have more and more to do. Aren't you going to the Junior High next fall? There you are. And it isn't fair to Teddy, either."

"Isn't it! Do *you* know what's fair to Teddy, huh?"

Uncle didn't pay any attention. "It may not be too late to teach Teddy something, Mrs. Breden says. She thinks he could learn a craft, so that he'll be useful. Wouldn't that be wonderful? If specialists have a chance to work with him and start him on the kind of thing he can manage and has the ability to do, he'd be much happier."

"He *is* happy. Teddy's always been happy. But when he's locked up, when you send him to prison, you're going to kill him . . . you . . ."

I couldn't get out all the words. I flew at Uncle and hammered and hammered at his waistcoat with my fists. Bang, bang, they went—he's hard.

"But, Mikkel." I was grabbed by the neck and thrown against the wall with a thump.

Father stood in front of me, his feet spread apart.

"What on earth's gotten into you? How dare you talk like that to Uncle Bjarne. And—and hitting him!"

"I didn't intend to say a word to Mikkel, but he

started asking questions. He just stood there and went on and on and . . ."

Father didn't listen to Uncle.

"Go to your room at once. And stay there! Don't come down again until you're prepared to apologize."

"Then I'll never come down!" I shouted, and dashed into the house.

I slammed the door and clumped upstairs as if I wanted to crush all the steps.

19

Waiting

I don't talk to anyone in the house.

Except when it's absolutely necessary.

I go to school, answer if I'm spoken to, do my homework, eat, sleep—a little, anyway.

Don't even talk to Teddy. Can't.

Nothing matters.

Mother tries to get around me and make me "happy" again. She brings me good things to eat and chats cheerfully when we're alone.

"You'll see how good it'll be for Teddy. We should be very happy that there are people who can help us."

"Happy!" And "help!"

No. Mother can save herself the trouble, and the scrambled eggs, too.

I stay in my room.

They're not going to talk me into believing that something wonderful is about to happen.

My silence is making Mother and Father nervous, I think.

Serves them right. Maybe they'll get a bad conscience, too, because they're betraying Teddy.

Sometimes Father is so bad-tempered that he looks as if he wants to throw me out the window. You're welcome. Just toss me.

"There's no reason to wander around looking like the plague. Pull yourself together, boy."

But Mother whispers and soothes him.

Teddy is up and well now.

He laughs and claps his hands when he sees me. Wants to play.

I won't. Can't.

So he hangs around Mother instead.

She hasn't asked me to help with him, even though she could use my help.

What's the point?

She'll soon have a rest from everything that's called Teddy.

She, who said she couldn't bear it if he were sent away!

Huh! Just pretending.

They don't think about anyone except themselves. Mother and Father and all the rest of them.

They make me sick.

Leif Arne and the boys have stopped asking me to play.

They only think of themselves, too. I wouldn't go

out anyway, not even if they asked me a hundred times.

They don't know how I feel inside.

No one knows. I sure feel low, all right.

Real, real low.

I've been low for a long time.

20

The Prison

Then one evening I heard what I'd been expecting
and fearing—Mother said that the next day they'd
take Teddy to Lillebo, to see if he liked it. "The
home we talked about, remember?"

Yes, thank you.

They would drive out with Father early in the
morning, before he went to work.

I spent the whole night thinking, and saw no way
out.

I only knew I'd have to go with them, no matter
what happened. I wanted to see for myself what it
was like at Lillebo, and where it was.

"See if he likes it . . ." They were clever, really
clever. I'd never thought Mother and Father would
be like that.

All they had to do was say, "Just imagine. Teddy
liked Lillebo so much that we let him stay there.

Isn't it wonderful? Forever. We'll never see him again. Isn't it wonderful?"

Great parents.

But they hadn't counted on Mikkel. He would go too, would look at Teddy's cell. Mikkel would find tools, and someday he'd break in and free Teddy.

I was prepared to yell and scream if they didn't allow me to go with them. But when I told them at the breakfast table that I'd decided to tag along, there were no protests.

"What about school?" asked Mother.

"I don't have any classes until the third period."

"Well, in that case"—Father planned to return to town immediately—"Mikkel can drive back with you, can't he?"

She got no answer from Father, who was gulping down his coffee. He shrugged his shoulders, mumbled something into his cup.

"Can't I do that?" I asked, stubborn and ready for battle.

"You might ask first, instead of just announcing your intentions."

But nobody said No, so it was all right.

I couldn't eat a thing—my throat was too tight. I couldn't even get a glass of milk down.

This was the last time Teddy would ever sit at the table. . . . No! I'd upset Uncle Bjarne's scheme!

Teddy had a good appetite. He didn't realize what was happening of course. He stuffed himself with cereal in great spoonfuls that lost a little of their load every time he carried them to his mouth. Plop, plop they fell on the plate.

"Ellik?" he said, with a smile and a big blob on his cheek, and I screwed my mouth into a smile too.

That made him even happier. He took a piece of bread from the basket and laid it on my plate with a kind "there-you-are—eat" nod.

Father left the table, and Mother buttered bread for his lunch. I put the piece back in the basket and went to get my school books.

They didn't put any baggage in the car. Father would probably drive it out in the evening when he'd seen how much Teddy "liked it."

The Volvo had been repaired and its front had been resprayed. It sputtered as usual. "The firm ought to buy new cars. It doesn't pay to drive a car as old as this one," said Father.

"Really," answered Mother, and looked as if she were thinking about something quite different.

We drove away with Teddy.

The rowan berries in the wood were a sour yellowish-red. They nodded in the wind, saying, "Bah! Hah! What did we say? Now you see how things have turned out. . . ."

"Num-a-num-num." Teddy rocked and sang and enjoyed himself during the drive.

Be clever, Teddy, and show them that you think the home is terrible. Scream, vomit, beat your head against the wall or something. Then I'll make a fuss, so you'll come home. Please, Teddy. Do it, I begged silently all the way there.

Lillebo—"fair view." A name like sugar icing. Enough to make you sick.

We saw the home after we'd driven for a good half hour.

It was quite an ordinary villa, not very big, sitting on a slope with maple trees around it.

It didn't exactly look like a prison. I couldn't see bars on any of the windows. But of course the cells might not be visible from the road.

"Look at the lovely garden!" Mother pointed. I saw a large lawn and a playground with a slide, a sand box, and swings.

"Um." Now Father was thinking about other things.

He parked outside the gate because it was shut. There was no barbed wire on top of the fence.

I'd hoped Teddy would sense something was wrong so he'd start to make trouble immediately. But he didn't. He padded along to the yard, without looking around.

A man was raking the red maple leaves into heaps.

"You . . . may . . . go . . . in." He bowed and turned away shyly but peered over his shoulder at us. He seemed to hope we would talk more to him. But then Mrs. Breden walked out the door.

Yes, Mrs. Breden herself, accompanied by a plump little lady in red overalls. So Mother and Father already knew Mrs. Breden. There was a lot that I didn't know.

". . . and this is the children's dear Auntie. In the

200

old days we used to work together in a special
school, and I think Lillebo is very lucky to have her
as its principal."

As Father and Mother greeted the principal—she
didn't look strict—Mrs. Breden turned to me.

"Hi, Mikkel. You managed to outfox me, after
all."

It was so odd. I didn't want to laugh. No one in
the world had less reason to laugh than I did. All
the same, my cheeks tugged at me so much that I
had to bite them to not smile back.

"You see, I phoned Malberg station and the hotel.
But nobody had seen two boys who looked as if they
were expecting an uncle who hadn't arrived." She
winked at me mischievously, but I pressed my lips
together, furious. I wanted to feel furious.

"No, I was too late. It took a while to get to the
boarding house, and then I had to put the children to
bed. The birds had flown from Malberg before I
returned."

Flown was the word. Mrs. Breden needn't look so
innocent. I knew enough to realize that she was
behind everything—she was the one who'd fooled
Mother and Father into bringing Teddy to Lillebo.

I liked her, though, but I didn't like liking her.

Now they wanted Teddy to go with them. Both
Mrs. Breden and the plump principal called him,
but he was only interested in the man with the rake.

They didn't talk to each other, but the man lent
Teddy the wooden rake, and Teddy tried to rake
leaves too.

"Hello, Teddy." Auntie went over to him and held out her hand.

Teddy looked at it and then at the rake. Finally he decided to let go of the rake and take the hand.

"Good morning. How nicely you greet people." Auntie snatched the rake handle as it fell, so it didn't conk the man on the head.

"You'll make friends with Oscar. He's our gardener. In the winter he carries wood and shovels snow and does a little of everything."

Oscar wriggled but lit up with a big grin. He did have some teeth in his mouth, but not many, although he didn't look much older than Father.

"Come inside, Teddy, and say hello to some more friends."

Teddy and the principal walked up the steps arm in arm. The rest of us followed, tense with excitement. It was no use wishing! Teddy didn't resist at all when he was led over the threshold.

The villa didn't look much like a prison inside either. We walked into a hall with a green fireplace and a broad staircase painted white. Along the wall big letters in different colors hung from hooks.

Auntie took a T and showed it to Teddy. "Here's your letter. You can take it with you, if you want to."

He hugged the T tightly and followed her.

The living room was too big. It was bright and quite pleasant, but the two long tables were also much too large. Only three children sat at one of them. They were busy playing with bricks, and drawing, but they looked up.

"These three children and a child who's ill live here permanently," Mrs. Breden whispered to Mother.

The largest girl got up and ran over to Auntie, hung on her arm, and told her a lot of things we didn't understand.

"Yes, indeed, Ellen. You're clever. Say 'Hello' to Teddy, now."

The girl peered at him cautiously; then she pulled Auntie's red apron over her face and hid in it, giggling.

A boy about my age wheeled himself over to us in a wheelchair and tugged at Teddy's jacket. "How nice," he said heartily. And "How nice," he went on saying.

Teddy stood still and sort of took in the atmosphere.

"You sit down beside Tone, Teddy." Mrs. Breden helped him sit down on a chair, gave him some bricks in the shape of letters, and told him to find one like his T.

Tone was terribly cross-eyed and had to twist her head over on one side to see Teddy. But she found him a T and threw it on the heap of bricks, and laughed loudly.

Teddy liked that. He took a brick also, threw it on the table, roared with laughter, and threw another. The boy who kept saying "How nice," wheeled himself after us, and all four of them sat there throwing bricks and laughing.

"Shush. The other children are coming." Auntie was trying to quiet them down.

Then I heard something that sounded like a phonograph record that was stuck. Two voices rose above the others, singing, "We sing as we go on our way."

I heard laughter and shouting, and children began to pour into the hall behind us. Two, four, five, eight —nine children. And two more if you counted an adult and an almost grown-up supervisor.

"This is the kindergarten supervisor, Aunt Vera, and her assistant, Liv," explained Mrs. Breden. Mother and Father nodded over all the heads, and the "aunts" smiled as they unbuttoned jackets and peeled satchels off children's shoulders.

The children varied a good deal in age and size, and Mrs. Breden told us that all of them had different kinds of injuries. She pulled us up on the stairs so we wouldn't get in the way of the children who were trying to hang up their own clothes.

Now, I thought. When Teddy sees all these children milling toward him, he'll certainly get frightened. Then he'll call for Ellik or Mother.

But Teddy let me down.

The children ran into the living room, which suddenly wasn't a bit too large, while Teddy stood beside Auntie and, like her, held out his arms to greet the children. He received them as if he were the host and everyone else were a guest. Some of them stopped and talked to Teddy, others walked past him and sat down. The adults helped the children who couldn't walk properly.

"We'll have to leave now, Mikkel."

"What?"

"Got to go now." Father was touching my arm.

"Go? But . . ." I was so confused. I didn't know what to think any more. "Can't we—shouldn't we say good-bye?"

"Better not bother the children. They're busy. You'll have to say good-bye for us, Jenny." Father lifted his hat and bowed to Auntie who waved back.

Then he told Mother quietly that he thought the bus would leave at half past three.

Not a word to Teddy, not a word about him! Father didn't look a bit sad.

He shook Mrs. Breden's hand vigorously. "Thank you so much for arranging for Teddy to be admitted."

"I didn't arrange a thing." Mrs. Breden laughed. "He has every right to be here. It was just a matter of speeding up the forms. It's wonderful that you live so nearby. There's not enough room to board more than the four children who are here, but you can drop Teddy every day."

Mother mumbled something and Father started walking, but I tried to put things straight inside my head. I felt very muddled. "Drop Teddy every day . . ."

"Good-bye, Mikkel. Why are you looking so surprised?"

How pretty Mrs. Breden looked. I had to give her a hug before I dashed off. Then it was her turn to look surprised.

"Come and see us sometime. Peik has been asking for you," she called after me.

"Father, Father, wait!" I sprinted past Oscar, making him drop his rake. "Sorry, good-bye—Father!"

"Yes, yes, what's the matter?" He unlocked the car door. He was late.

"Teddy's coming back home? Are you sure? Teddy'll come back for dinner every day?"

"Why shouldn't he?"

"I thought . . ." I flopped down on the car seat, panting. "Thought . . . he would . . . live here. Not come home."

Father turned on the ignition, but the engine stalled because he forgot about the choke. "So that's what you thought."

Father would never let anyone down. "I'm sorry," I said.

"That's okay. I understand now. But don't forget Uncle—"

"I'll tell Uncle I'm sorry."

"Fine."

Father drove me to school. I told anyone who would listen that Teddy was going to school too.

"How can he go to school?" asked Karsten.

"It's a special school for children with brain injuries. They have specialists who teach them the kind of things they can manage. . . ." I heard Uncle's words coming out of my mouth.

I felt just like a clock that had been standing still for a long time because it hadn't been wound up. Now everything began to tick. All my wheels started turning. The gang looked relieved to see me acting normally again. They grinned.

"Aren't you mad any more?" Leif Arne didn't sound a bit mad himself, although he had good reason to be.

The ball team agreed to meet the next day for a workout, because the Biters wanted to replay the game, since we'd scrapped the last one.

If Stig comes, I thought, I'll say I'm sorry about his teeth. But I'll knock down anyone who pesters my brother, teeth or no teeth. Well, maybe that wouldn't be a good idea.

I'll tell everyone who thinks Teddy should be locked up that he's going to school now. He's going to walk to the bus and back every day. That's what I'll tell them.

21

"Pippurra!"

I was home from school. Mother was about to put Teddy to bed. Father was counting his money on the table. Today was his payday.

"I have almost a hundred *kroner,*" I said. "We can go halves on the dentist's bill."

"Eh? Money? Weren't you planning to buy skiis?"

He put a pile of notes in Mother's housekeeping box.

"A youngster like you shouldn't have that big a responsibility. It was wrong of us to ask you to take care of Teddy so much."

There. He'd finally taken it away from me—the responsibility. But I didn't like that, either.

"I'm not as little as you think, even if I look little."

"Um, no. Maybe that's true." Father chewed sideways as he glanced at me. "Did you go to Uncle Bjarne?"

"Yes, he was very decent. He thought I knew more about Lillebo than I did, of course. Thought you'd told me that Teddy would only go there during the day."

"Um, should have told you, sure. But you carried on about everything. We thought we'd talk about it later."

And he explained that they'd thought that Uncle had told me. Besides, they'd had so many other things to think about and discuss and fix that there hadn't been much time for sitting and talking.

When Mother came in, the three of us talked, like grownups.

We agreed that Mother would take Teddy to the bus every morning and I would pick him up in the afternoon. The supervisor called Aunt Vera rode on the same bus and looked after the children.

Mother told us how the teachers played with the children at Lillebo and taught them at the same time. She said a speech therapist gave classes twice a week.

Teddy and the other children were going to do gymnastics too. They would get a different teacher for that. And later on Teddy would be examined by doctors and specialists to find out what he could learn and what he was capable of doing.

This was what Uncle Bjarne had been trying to tell us for years. But until recently there hadn't been a Lillebo near us, and even though Dr. Brun and the Child Welfare Council had said that Teddy needed treatment, they hadn't been able to find room for him. They'd seemed happy that Mother could keep him at home.

"Now he can stay with us forever. And no one will bother us?"

Mother looked out the window. Father cleared his throat. So they did know more than I knew.

"Forever?" asked Mother. "We won't live forever, of course."

"I shall. I mean, not forever, but longer than Teddy, anyway."

"Have you got that in writing, Mikkel?" asked Father. "A car might run over you."

That was true. People don't always live longer than their older brothers and sisters.

"We'll just have to do our best to see that he can manage on his own."

Mother nodded. Oscar, whom we'd met, was alone in the world, she said. But he'd been lucky enough to accompany Auntie from the former home to Lillebo. There weren't too many jobs like Oscar's. "The more Teddy learns, the more opportunities he'll have in the future. Later on they may decide that he can't get enough instruction at Lillebo, and then . . ." Mother didn't continue.

"What then?"

"Well, then we'll have to let him go wherever people can best help him."

"But why aren't there more schools like Lillebo

and workshops around here? Our teacher says that more are needed in our country."

"Money, money. They cost so much."

"If we had a lot of money, we could pay teachers to come here and teach Teddy at home, couldn't we?"

That wouldn't be possible, Father said. You needed equipment, rooms, material. There was a shortage of trained people too—specialists and doctors and nurses. No, it wasn't so simple. "But they go on collecting funds and handing them out, so things are bound to improve. And a lot of countries are worse off than we are."

"Do you think that someday there'll be enough money and people so we wouldn't have to send Teddy away?"

Father didn't know. "But I'll tell you something. We've been thinking too much about ourselves in this house. We've just looked at everything from our point of view."

"Oh?" He was saying what I used to believe. But in a different way.

He said we'd only thought about what it would mean to *us* if we didn't have Teddy. We'd thought how much *we'd* miss him. Of course, we'd thought he would be unhappy without us. Now we'd seen that he might not be unhappy, Father said. That was true. Mother and Father had met some parents at Mrs. Breden's house—imagine, they'd gone to her house!—whose child was in a home, and he was even younger than Teddy.

211

They'd said it was hard at first. But when they saw how much their child learned and how much happier he seemed, they were grateful that they'd made the decision.

"We'll just have to learn to decide what's best for Teddy," agreed Mother.

"Ellik!" called Teddy from his bedroom. He'd sensed that we were friends again, so he followed me around the house all the time.

I went into his room, and Mother and Father followed me.

He was sitting up in bed, with Winnie-the-Pooh in his arms. "How nice!" We recognized the hearty voice and expression and laughed.

We sang the teddy bear song with him, sitting on the edge of the bed. It turned into rather a mixed chorus, like the chorus of the children at Lillebo.

But we waited, laughed, waited, as his smile got broader, and then . . .

Teddy clapped his hands.

"Pippurra!"

29505 HARRIET TUBMAN: *Conductor on the Underground Railroad,* by Ann Petry. A woman of great moral courage, Harriet Tubman led over three hundred black men, women, and children from slavery to freedom on the dangerous escape route to the North. (75¢)

29261 THREE ON THE RUN, by Nina Bawden. Frontispiece illustration by Wendy Worth. Sudden adventure grips Ben, Lil, and their African friend, Thomas Okapi, as they are plunged into an international plot and must make a wild desperate flight from London. (60¢)

29289 LIGHT A SINGLE CANDLE, by Beverly Butler. When Cathy lost her sight at the age of fourteen, she had to abandon her dreams of being an artist. But with the help of a guide dog, a new life of independence and promise opens up for her. (60¢)

29258 HILLS END, by Ivan Southall. Illustrated by Jim Phillips. Cut off from all adult help, surrounded by wild mountains and a flooded river, seven boys and girls fight for survival on their own. (60¢)

29268 WAYFARING LAD, by Ivy Bolton. Illustrated by Lorence F. Bjorklund. Sixteen-year-old Richard Nolan takes a perilous journey alone through the frontier territory of Tennessee— when the fierce Chickamaugas are on the war path. (60¢)

29038 RUN, WESTY, RUN, by Gudrun Alcock. Illustrated by W. T. Mars. Westy hates his room without windows, his street without trees, and the crabby grocer he works for. One day he makes a break for what he hopes will bring freedom, space and privacy. (50¢)

29297 HOW MANY MILES TO BABYLON? by Paula Fox. Illustrated by Paul Giovanopoulos. Three tough kids kidnap James to use him in their dog-stealing racket. But James plans a daring and courageous escape. (60¢)

29504 CHILDREN OF THE RESISTANCE, by Lore Cowan. Eight dramatic, true stories of teen-agers who fought for freedom in the underground resistance movement in Europe during World War II. (75¢)

29506 CAVE OF DANGER, by Bryce Walton. When Matt discovers a big, new cave, he and his friend make the risky descent underground and plunge straight into terrifying adventure. (75¢)

29041 THE STRANGE INTRUDER, by Arthur Catherall. A reign of terror grips a remote, storm-lashed island when a dangerous invader comes ashore. (50¢)

(If your bookseller does not have the titles you want, you may order them by sending the retail price, plus 25¢ for postage and handling to: Mail Service Department, POCKET BOOKS, a division of Simon & Schuster, Inc., 1 West 39th Street, New York, N. Y. 10018. Please enclose check or money order—do not send cash.)

29524